THE
IMMUNDUS

Odolf Mingan

THE
IMMUNDUS

CHRISTINA ENQUIST

Odolf Mingan

Odolf Mingan

ODOLF MINGAN PUBLISHING
5211 W. GOSHEN AVE., STE. 158 VISALIA, CA 93291

Visit our website at www.odolfminganpublishing.com

Book design by Rachel Lawston

The text for this book is set in Adobe Garamond Pro

PUBLISHER'S CATALOGING-IN-PUBLICATION DATA

(Prepared by The Donohue Group, Inc.)

Names: Enquist, Christina.

Title: The Immundus / Christina Enquist.

Description: Visalia, CA : Odolf Mingan, [2017] | Series: [The Immundus series] ; [book 1] | Interest age level: 12 and up. | Summary: Nia Luna is a 16-year-old geneticist apprentice living in Domus in the year 2828. Domus is the last chance for mankind to escape extinction. When the Immundus threaten the citizens of Domus, Nia is forced to face the Immundus from outside the city and from within.

Identifiers: ISBN 9780999414002 (hardcover) | ISBN 9780999414019 (paperback) | ISBN 9780999414026 (ebook)

Subjects: LCSH: Human beings--Juvenile fiction. | Geneticists--Juvenile fiction. | Extinction (Biology)--Juvenile fiction. | Imaginary places--Juvenile fiction. | Speculative fiction. | CYAC: Human beings--Fiction. | Geneticists--Fiction. | Extinction (Biology)--Fiction. | Imaginary places--Fiction.

Classification: LCC PZ7.1.E56 Im 2017 (print) | LCC PZ7.1.E56 (ebook) | DDC [Fic]--dc23

For my son, Nicholas Carrillo, who has been such a gift in my life; my husband, Kevin, who keeps me sane; my mother, Linda Matus, who would do anything for me; my dad, Arturo Matus, for not only being there when I was a single parent, but also for imparting a love for all aspects of the arts; and my sister, Monica, for helping me with Nicholas when I was on my own.

This is also for my grandmothers who were instrumental in my life and who are no longer with us: Christine Dominguez Matus and Jesusa Ruiz Montes.

ACKNOWLEDGEMENTS

I would like to thank my husband, my alpha reader, for his patience and understanding as I spent nights and weekends writing and editing. Also, Season Burch, Pattie Godfrey-Sadler, L.R. Johnson, and Dorinda Judd of the Inspired Writers League for your support and friendship. For the many beta readers that helped shape my story: Chase Burch, Shawndra Johnson, Paul Bishop, Amber Hall, Saundra Luchs, Sylvia Curry, Whitney Tolman, Alexia Travis, and Serena Corrales. Sorry if I missed anyone. And, of course, my wonderful group during the Storymakers Publication Primer: Elana Johnson, Jeigh Meredith, Susan Knight, Ruth Morris, and Ranee S. Clark. My amazing editors Katrina Diaz Arnold and Parisa Zolfaghari. Book and cover designer Rachel Lawston for her brilliant creativity. COS Productions for their amazing work on the book trailers. Laura Flavin and Emily Mullen for marketing and publicity, respectively. Simon Appleby and the Bookswarm team for a fabulous author website. And my family and friends for cheering me on and always having faith in me.

But I say unto you, Love your enemies, bless them that curse you, do good to them that hate you, and pray for them which despitefully use you and persecute you.

Matthew 5:44

PART ONE

IN THE BEGINNING THERE WAS DARKNESS

ONE

COLOSSEUM

The refrigerator is bare and broken, unable to order the fruits and vegetables we are missing. I was hoping to eat something before the game. My father is working and probably won't be home until I'm already asleep, so I'll have to go to the commissary before the game. It's times like these I miss my mom. Today, June 8, 2828 is the anniversary of her unexpected departure. It's been four years of trickling lamentation. A murky feeling casts a shadow on my heart, like the clouds looming outside.

Why would the climatologist program clouds for game day? I push the thought away. Maybe they'll dissipate by game time. I run back in the house, grabbing my jacket from the living room sofa.

I walk to my car. Her doors open when I get close enough for her to recognize my microchips, embedded throughout my body at birth.

"Hello, Nia," she greets me, a smile in her tone as she revs her engine.

"Hi, Jules," I slide into the front seat. She must be fully sun-powered because her tone is grumpy when she's running low. "Display commissary collection history." I listen attentively as Jules recites my purchase history. "Resubmit the last order, then take me to the commissary."

Suddenly, an image of Mom preparing rice pilaf with sautéed mushrooms and garlic plants itself in my mind. The memory so vivid I can taste the garlic and smell her scent—a bouquet of jasmine, rose, and lavender, with a bottom note of vanilla. A lump in my throat restricts air to my lungs and my chest tightens.

A face, a common one, one that I've seen a thousand times, appears on the dash screen. "Immundus have been sighted along the eastern wall near Genesis. Guards have been deployed. All streets from Johnson to Burch will be closed to traffic and pedestrians. All citizens in the Mission district must remain indoors." I cage my breath. "The Spero match in the Tower District will remain scheduled as planned." My breath escapes with relief. *At least the game is still happening. I wonder if the drill instructor will work us harder tomorrow. I see fifty push-ups in my future.*

"Jules, play Spero playlist."

· · ● ● ● · ·

It's a fifteen-minute drive to the commissary, which allows enough time for them to pull the order together. The drive-through is not as packed as I expected. Only two cars wait in front of me. I tell Jules to lower the music volume as we approach the 3D hologram woman.

"Good morning, Nia! Your order will be ready by the time you reach the door."

Each person, child, and adult in Domus receives two hundred food credits for the month; each item collected is worth one credit since all food is valued equally. There are no bulk items, just individual items. We're paid the first of the month. I have 180 food credits left after this collection. It takes a few minutes before I make it to the 4D hologram door. My cart of food comes out the door and hovers around to the back of Jules, who already has her trunk open. Her long metallic trunk arms reach out, grab the bags from the cart, and pull them in.

"Groceries are secure," Jules says, closing her trunk and pulling away. I catch a glimpse of the cart in the rearview mirror, returning through the door.

Four twenty-five p.m. displays on Jules's screen. I still have plenty of time to make it to the game. My eyes linger too long on the date— reminding me again of my mother and how I felt at twelve.

She left at the end of my first year in school. I remember being excited to tell Mom I was going to play in the Spero games the next year, expecting to come home to a warm house, a smile, and a "How was your day, honey." Instead, I found the house eerily quiet and dark, shades drawn. No warmth. No smile. No words. Just a black hole of silence. "Mom?" I shouted. Silence greeted me. "Mom, are you home?"

I walked into the kitchen, thinking that she must have gone to the store. On the table was a small folded sheet of paper with the word "Nia" written in her handwriting on the front. I opened it and read the first words: "Nia, I love you!" I still remember feeling sunshine in the pit of my stomach. My mom was the only person who said "I love you" to me. I don't know why my father never said it—still doesn't, even though I'm the only one left in our family.

I continued reading: "Please know that what I am doing is because of this love for you. I want to keep you safe. I'm sorry I can't say more. I'm leaving. But know that I will always be with you, in your heart."

A million questions flooded my mind like a raging river with nothing to impede its current. *Safe from what? Leaving? Why? What does this mean? You can't leave me, too.* I'd just lost my best friend, Fiducia, three years prior to that moment. As if my body knew the pain before my mind did, I remember falling to my knees, my body bent forward, and gripping at the bamboo flooring. A sharp pain radiated through my stomach, replacing the warmth felt seconds prior. Every muscle in my body constricted as though in the grasp of a python. My head grew light and a buzzing began in my ears as the world around me became enshrouded in a thick fog.

The next thing I remember was my father waking me two hours later. I realized then that I must have passed out. I looked up at my father. He had just arrived from work—the note dangled from his fingers. His eyes reflected anguish, his eyebrows drawn in, and his skin sallow.

"Sam, replay Rosemary's last moments here," he said. Sam, our house, had a hologram interface that could take the shape of a man or woman, depending on user preference. We had programmed her as an older woman, around her eighties.

Sam appeared and morphed into my mother, per my father's request. I watched as my mom placed every letter on the note, but I couldn't bear to watch anymore. I had run upstairs to my bedroom, while my father replayed the video over and over again.

My heart shrank into itself then, a deep melancholy encumbering my body and mind. I couldn't speak or sleep or scream. All I could do was feel. Feel the loss. Feel the heartache. Feel the pain. I lost my mom.

I didn't understand my mom's choice then and I don't understand it now. Both my father and I have been tormented by her decision, and neither of us have been able to console the other. Since she left, life has held a void for me.

I increase the volume of the music again and it drowns out my memories.

· · • ● • · ·

I arrive at The Colosseum, known as the AT&T stadium in the Genus Guadiam history books. A myriad of colorful attire adorns the eager spectators already forming at the front entrance.

"Jules, drop me off at the player entrance, then go home to deliver the groceries. Sam is expecting them."

The game starts at seven o'clock and it's the only one for the entire quarter, so everyone gets there early. The four teams spend all quarter gearing up to play against each other and the tension is noticeable. My team consists of Eric, Alex, and Casey. We're the Cogs from the School of Cognition. The team from Genus Voluptas is called the Affects; the ones from the School of Physiology, the Physos; and the fourth from the School of Sociology is the Soshes.

"What took you so long?" A voice booms from the distance. I shield the sun from my eyes and make out that it's Eric at the player's entrance door. It's open a quarter, just enough for him to have his feet planted in the building with his body leaning outside, one hand against the door frame and the other on the door knob. I trot toward the door. I can feel my ponytail swaying back and forth with every footfall.

"I stopped at the commissary." He opens the door wider to let me in. The colosseum halls are a light beige and wrap around the outer edge of the colosseum, branching out into rooms, lockers, and offices. Our locker room is around the bend.

"You? Why didn't you have Jules go to the commissary after she dropped you off?"

"Yeah. I guess I could have done that. I have a lot on my mind."

"That's right." Eric's voice sounds hollow. He has been my best friend since I started school, which was only shortly after Fiducia died, and before my mom abandoned my father and I. So he was there for me during all my emotional swings, from "life is great" to "life is hell"— and never dissed me for it. He never forgets. "Are you going to be able to keep your head in the game or should we call for your backup?"

"I can play. I need this distraction."

"It needs to mean more to you than a distraction if we're going to win."

I grab his arm and stop him mid-step. "I've got this." I cross my arms, fists to shoulders. "I promise." He smiles and nods in acceptance.

In the locker room, Casey and Alex are already in their uniforms, sitting on a bench, talking. Our school colors are black and blue, so the uniforms are black, form-fitting jumpsuits, with wide blue stripes running up the left and right sides. The back of the uniform mirrors the front, except for the zipper that goes down the center from the neck to the small of our backs.

Casey spots me and swings her legs over the bench, away from Alex, and walks toward me. Her hands grasp my shoulders. "Are you doing okay? I was worried we were going to have to call your backup."

"Yeah. I just had to stop at the commissary to get some food."

"Your fridge isn't linked to Jules?"

"The fridge is broken and the mechbot that usually handles those repairs is out of commission, too."

"Why didn't you just send Jules?"

"I know, I already heard that from Eric."

Coach Brisbane, a squat man, bellows out, "Casey! Leave her be." Swinging his finger between Eric and I, he continues, "You two hurry up and get dressed. We have twenty minutes before we have to be on the field."

I make my way to the changing room and quickly dress, wondering the entire time what obstacles the gamers and audience have planned for us this time. The gamers give the audience obstacle options to choose from for each player. So whatever we experience it's because the audience selected it.

I step out of the changing area and take a seat next to Eric.

"Is your dad coming to the game this quarter?" Alex asks, causing Casey to nudge him in the ribs with her elbow. She can do that because they've been dating for two years.

"No," I choke out. My father couldn't care less about my games—he's never been to one. We used to attend the Spero games as a family when Mom was around, but since she left, he spends most his waking hours in his lab. The only time we ever really talk is in the morning because I'm asleep when he gets home—if he gets home. There've been countless nights when I've left dinner for him on the counter, but it's still there in the morning. Untouched.

Coach gives a short motivational speech and finishes right before the bell rings, letting us know we have five minutes to be on the field, so we trek over to our starting positions. The colosseum is a bright white. I stare up at the colorful spectators sitting in their chairs with their odd-looking glasses that allow them to choose the obstacles and zoom in on a specific player they want to watch; they also have the option of choosing different viewpoints or angles, and the spectator can even watch the game from the viewpoint of one of the players. They're probably reviewing all the obstacle options, eager to make their selections when the game starts.

The referee along with three other women approach us on the field, placing an earwrap around our ears. The earwrap allows the referees to communicate with us. They use a unique adhesive to make sure it stays on throughout the game. After the game, it washes off with a special liquid. Nothing else will remove the adhesive. I've tried.

The four dimension holographic maze begins to take form filling the entire field of the stadium. The smooth cream-colored floor takes form first. It's as though a layer of coconut cream was spread across the green field. The walls sprout next, a sea of light gray with small black dots speckled throughout the walls—cameras. I see the first obstacle appear near the entrance of the maze. The maze has an obstacle course strewn throughout, designed to test instinct, intelligence, agility, strength, and creativity. The team that makes it to the other side of the maze first wins.

If a player fails to overcome an obstacle or if the timer runs out for a teammate, then the entire team loses and the maze provides exits for the losing teammates. Every quarter, coach reminds us of that rule, so we understand that a team is only as good as its weakest player. When we train, we help each teammate build their talents and strengths, rather than focusing on our own development. If three of the four teams fail, then the remaining team in the maze wins by default without having to make it to the other side of the maze. My team has won almost every year, and one-third of our wins are by default.

"Here we go!" says Eric, looking at me as he hits his left palm with his fist.

When I first volunteered to participate in Spero, it was for fun. But the moment I first played, I realized what an escape it was—a temporary release from the constant ache in my heart. I mask the pain from the world, but Spero is the only time I can mask it from myself.

Each team begins to make their way to the south entrance of the maze. The other teams' uniforms are analogous in design to our own but distinguishable by their school colors. Soshes in apple red and black, Affects in lime green and black, and the Physos in silver and black.

A line appears at the entrance informing us where to start. We position ourselves at the line, my teammates to my right, and the other teams to my left. We wait, anxiously anticipating the bell that will alert us to begin. Seconds feel like minutes as I wait, my frenetic heart already barreling forward. My hands are clammy, and my eyes fixate on the first obstacle. If a player runs prior to the bell, the team is immediately eliminated.

The bell sounds.

And we're off.

T W O

SPERO

We surge—a wave of bodies stampeding toward the first obstacle. A Soshe bumps my arm as I run past her. Four players are ahead of me, but one of them is Eric. I arrive at the first obstacle, a contorted mess of wood that we have to get through. *Agility.* I spot a spiral-shaped section of the wood to squeeze through. On my left, I catch a glimpse of Eric climbing over the wooden structure as an Affect tries to pull him down. I hurl my body up and into the spiral opening, slinking my way through. Even with the uniform, I feel the roughness of the wood. I spot Casey to my right, making her way through a hole in the jumble wood as well. I don't see Alex, though.

"Ten seconds," the referee announces in the earpiece.

Adrenaline bursts throughout my body and in three large thrusts I finally reach the end, stretching my arms to the ground and somersaulting to the floor. Players are scattering into all four of the possible routes. Then the maze shifts. Now instead of four possible routes ahead of me, there are two, left or right, with a solid wall in front of me. Five other players, including Casey, are faced with the same option. This is new—the gamers haven't done this before.

"I'll go left," Casey says adamantly, sweat already beading up on her brow.

"Okay." I nod in affirmation.

My head snaps back and I yell out in pain. Someone had pulled me back by my ponytail. When I turn around to see who it is, I feel a foot swipe underneath mine. I collapse to the floor, my butt and elbows getting the brunt of the impact. I look ahead to see who pulled me down—a Soshe. I look down for a moment processing what just happened, then take a deep breath. I jump back up, adrenaline searing my skin. I sprint to the Soshe, tackling her to the ground. A crimson river gushes from her nose, spattering across the cream-colored ground. I wasn't expecting that.

"I'm sorry," I say, feeling guilty for drawing blood.

The maze shifts again, presenting me with three routes where there was initially one. My head feels dizzy from the shifting of the maze, and I wonder how I'm going to get to the other end if it continues shifting. I take the route in the middle, glancing back to see if anyone is behind me—it's clear. A hologram of a woman appears, along with three doors.

"Beyond one of the doors is a test of your creativity. The other two will kick you out of the game."

Instinct.

"You have ten seconds to decide."

I close my eyes and steady my racing mind, knowing that my decision could cost the game. I step to the middle door. Slowly curling my fingers around the handle, I open it and step into a room. The door disappears into the wall. There is a small table in the corner. On the table lays a candle, a box of thumbtacks, and a book of matches.

The referee announces, "The Soshes have been removed from the Maze." I sigh, relief spilling through my body. *Two teams left.*

The same female hologram reemerges saying, "Affix the candle, while lit, to the wall, ensuring that no wax drips on the table."

I pick up the candle and a thumbtack. *How am I supposed to use this tiny thumbtack to stick the candle to the wall?* I look at all the items, picturing different ways in my mind, until I realize I can use the large box that the thumbtacks are in to hold the candle. I dump the thumbtacks on the table and place the candle into it to make sure it fits—it does. I pin the box to the wall, place the candle in it, then light the candle. The room and table dissipate, a route taking its place.

In the distance, there are several routes shooting off from this one route, like branches from a tree. I run down the route, slowing to a jog as I approach the first set of paths. I peer left and right, looking for others, but I see no one. I wonder if the gamers are leaving me alone as punishment since I caused the Soshe to bleed. I take a few more steps along the route I'm on and peer into some other branches. Still no one. Rather than continue to check all divergent paths ahead, I take a path to the right. The maze shifts. I hold my unsettled stomach and look back, but a wall stands from where I came. In front of me, a female hologram appears. The ground beneath her becomes water for what seems like a quarter of a mile. Just as a motorboat manifests, she says, "You must bring the bag of grain, the chicken, and the fox across to the other side of the water." She points to my right where hologram versions of these things appear. "But you can only carry one at a time."

I reach my foot toward the water curious to see how deep it is, but I stop myself, realizing I might disqualify my team. I glance over at the bag of grain, the chicken, and the fox. The animals are just as I remember them from the animal museum, but are currently motionless. I figure once I make a selection, the chicken and fox will somehow activate, making the task more difficult. If I take the fox over and leave the chicken with the grain, the chicken will undoubtedly break into the bag and eat the grain, and if I take the grain over first and leave the fox with the chicken, then the fox will get the chicken. But if I take the chicken over first, the fox could care less about the grain, so I guess I'm taking the chicken over first.

I grab the chicken, which begins squawking and flapping its feathers. When I step into the motorboat with the chicken, the fox awakens, pacing back and forth at the edge of the water. There is nowhere for the fox to go since a wall blocks him from escaping. I travel to the other side, struggling to hold on to the chicken as it wrestles with me. Its feathers are soft and slippery, reminding me of a blanket at home. Almost there . . .

almost there. I drop the chicken off on the small piece of maze. There is nowhere for the chicken to go either since a wall keeps it near the edge of the water. "Ten minutes," chimes the referee.

I return quickly to the fox and grain. *Now which do I take?* If I take the fox and drop it off, it will probably eat the chicken. If I take the grain, then the chicken will dig into the bag and eat the grain. I'm back to the problem I had initially. *Ugh!* What if I keep one in the boat with me to keep them separate? If I take the grain over and then bring the chicken back and get the fox, then the fox and the grain will be on the other side with the chicken on the original side. *Yes! That's what I'll do.* Without getting out of the boat, I reach for the bag of grain, dragging it into the motorboat.

When I reach the other side, I lift the bag of grain onto the ground and grab the chicken as it approaches the bag. I reach the original side, drop off the chicken and quickly grab the fox before it attacks the chicken. The fox's fur is softer than the chicken's feathers and not as agitated as the chicken. It relaxes on my lap the entire ride. I arrive at the other side and drop off the fox. Halfway to the originating side the referee announces, "Three minutes." I speed up, grab the chicken, and make it to the other side before time is up. The moment I plant both feet on the ground near the now motionless fox and chicken, they disappear and three routes appear in front of me. Behind me lay a pure white path where the water was. "Congratulations!" The referee announces, a smile in his voice.

I can't help but grin. I take the middle path, running about ten paces into the route when a pole materializes in front of me. I wait for the hologram to appear to tell me what I'm supposed to do with the pole. A ceiling appears throughout my route. A breeze fills the hall, growing stronger each second. I grab the pole when the force of the wind pushes my body. My feet slide from the now-hurricane wind. I close my tear-filled eyes. My body lifts into the air, parallel to the floor, my legs undulating like a flag in the wind. I grip the pole tightly, one hand above the other. A cramping pain shoots through my hands. *Do not let go. Do not let go. Do not let go.*

The moment I feel I might not be able to hold on any longer, the winds cease, allowing my body to fall to the floor. I massage my stiff hands.

The ceiling recedes and the pole retracts, leaving me in an empty room with a door on three sides. *How do I escape a constant changing maze?* An Affect walks in, followed by a Physo. The female hologram appears, transporting us to a snow-covered field. It's beautiful. In the distance there are trees—lots of trees—and a winding babbling creek. I reach down, allowing the snow to slide through my fingers, numbing my skin and radiating pain through the bones of my hand. How could something so beautiful cause such pain?

"You are in a harsh environment," says the hologram. "It is twenty-five degrees below zero, but at nighttime it will be below forty."

The air doesn't match what we are being told.

"The nearest town is twenty miles away. Based on this information, you must use the following items to stay alive."

The hologram points to a table with eleven items appearing before us. They are a stringy-looking sponge made of metal, a laser blade, a cymbal, a battery, a large jar of coconut oil with a very shiny metal lid, a strainer, three large rolls of plain paper, extra clothes for each of us, a twenty-by-twenty-foot piece of heavy duty canvas, a compass, and three bananas. "You have twenty minutes to devise a plan to determine in what order and for what purpose you will use the items. If you do not choose correctly, all teams lose."

"*All* teams lose?" The Physo repeats, snarling.

"What kind of game is this?" The Affect chimes in. The hologram disappears. I glance over at the Affect and Physo.

"Does anyone have any ideas on what paper can be used for?" The Physo asks, one eyebrow arched up.

"It can be used to stay warm when bundled around the body underneath one's clothes," replies the Affect in her singsong voice. "In history class, we watch classic shows and I've seen this technique used more than once."

"I love shows. She's right. I've seen that, also," I respond. I want to contribute something, so I say, "Bananas can be used . . ."

"Isn't that obvious! It's what we eat," the Physo interjects with his stentorian voice, his tone demeaning.

"If you let me finish, you would learn that we could also use the banana peels to filter the creek water since we need to stay hydrated," I argue. His beady eyes and curled mouth reveal his dissatisfaction.

"That's pretty cool!" says the Affect. At least one of them seems to be affable. Her comment gives me enough confidence to make another suggestion.

"I think the important thing to consider is that we're supposedly freezing right now. What else can we use beside the paper to stay warm?"

"The battery and the steel wool," the Physo responds. "We rub the battery against the steel wool until it catches on fire, but we'll need to use the laser blade to cut down some of those trees for wood first, so we can place the steel wool on the wood to give us a large fire."

Our discussion continues and before we realize it, time has passed. "Five minutes remain," rings in my ear. We glance at each other and finalize what we are going to tell the hologram.

I realize that even if we choose correctly, if one of the other teams gets it wrong, we are all out. This didn't make sense to me. Why would the gamers add this type of challenge and this type of consequence where there might not be a winner? The Physo shares our plan with the hologram.

"Congratulations!" The hologram announces as the maze returns us to the room where we started.

Smiles are uncaged at our victory. My heart still racing as we wait to find out if the other teams passed. Three routes suddenly appear. We're safe. Without saying another word, each of us takes a separate path.

I take a path that seems to lead to a dead end, but as I get closer I notice at the end I can turn left or right. As I turn right, I bump into Alex around the corner.

"Oops. Sorry!" he says with a flushed face.

"Fancy meeting you here," I say facetiously.

"What's down the way you came?"

"I just finished a team—" A wall appears between Alex and I.

"No conversing in the game," the referee announces through my earpiece, "unless you are working on a team challenge, which you currently are not."

I turn around and jog down the path. A hologram appears. Around ten feet of the floor in front of me disappears, leaving a large black hole. Small square stepping-stones appear in zig-zag formation, hovering over nothing and level with the floor.

"You have ten seconds to make it across without falling." I look down into pitch black. There must be something down there. The gamers wouldn't risk our lives.

"On the count of three, I will say *go*. Are you ready?"

"Yes," I say, narrowing my gaze on the stones.

"One . . . Two . . . Three . . . Go!"

My left foot hits the first stone, second, third, zig-zagging across when I hear, "The Affects have been removed from the Maze." Distracted, my footing is not secure on the next stone and I start sliding off the edge, but I am moving so fast that I don't lose my balance, and manage to make it across.

Two holograms appear with varying heights and builds—both larger than me.

"You must fight each hologram," the referee announces.

I approach the female, receiving a swift kick to the jaw, knocking me down onto my hands and knees. Blood swells in my mouth, some spilling to the floor. *I suppose I deserved that since I drew blood earlier.* I spit and push myself up to standing position.

I circle the hologram that punched me, from a distance, fists up. I punch the female, but my fist slides through. "That's not fair!" I yell up and out toward the crowd.

"You have to be faster than—" I swing my arms violently hitting her stomach and ribs.

The other hologram holds his ground. My knuckles tense and ache. Even with the daily morning combat training that prepares us for a possible war against the Immundus, the conditioning does not diminish the pain. Every citizen of Domus, eleven and older, is considered military. Her fist digs into my side, the side that is still slightly bruised, where a stick pole was jammed the week prior, causing me to scream out. I grab her head, ram it to my knees, and kick her in the stomach, forcing her to fall back against the other hologram—sending both to the ground. They disappear on impact.

"You now have five minutes to exit the maze."

I never made it this far without the other teams losing. I run feverishly through the one route given. I slip around one of the corners but rise swiftly. *I can't let my team down. I can't let my team down. I can't let my team down.*

"Two minutes to exit the maze."

I hear the drumming of my heart in my ears, beating faster than my feet are taking me. A stream of sweat rolls down one of my cheeks, skimming my mouth. Salty. A sudden tinge of thirst occupies my throat.

"One minute to exit the maze."

An aching pain makes itself known on the right side of my abdomen, as though my insides are twisting. *Are my teammates done and waiting for me? What if I'm the reason we lose?* I reach another corner—gentler this time. Please let this be the way out. With one foot around the corner, the maze disintegrates. The remaining players scattered throughout the field. It looks like no one made it out of the maze.

"The Gamers won!" The referee's voice boomed across the stadium.

How can the gamers win? They control the maze—they weren't playing. Were they? And if they were, why weren't we informed?

THREE

SCHOOL

From my upstairs bedroom, I hear a knock on my front door, but I trust Sam to answer. She used to have the ability to scan the chips of visitors, but with my dad so consumed with work, he hasn't gotten around to getting a new mechbot to handle the repairs. I would do it myself, but bots are not allowed to be purchased by anyone under the age of twenty-one.

"Who, may I ask, is seeking entrance?"

"Nia's knight in shining armor," Eric replies.

"Nia. Your knight in shining armor is at the door," Sam announces.

I roll my eyes. "Sam, tell him I'm coming down." I pull my hair into a ponytail, then dash downstairs, my hair brushing the nape of my neck. Through the door, I see him in his jeans and T-shirt. The door disintegrates as I approach. Eric's standing there with a smirk on his face, enjoying his comment.

"Your Tesla awaits," he says, gesturing toward his cherry red car. As we near his car, the door dissipates, and a glint of sunlight from the solar panels on the car pokes my eyes. I slide into a seat.

· · • ● • · ·

Eric rubs the back of his neck, darts a gaze at me, then rests his eyes on his hands.

"So . . ." he starts, his hands unable to find peace, wrestling with each other as if one could find dominance over the other. Something is definitely on his mind.

"What?" I ask, my heart beating to the rhythm of a drum roll in anticipation of what he's struggling to say.

Spit it out, Eric.

His car starts driving. He's already programmed the autopilot to take us to school. Today's our last day. The day we find out where we will serve our apprenticeship for the next five years.

He looks up at me with a strangeness in his eyes. "I saw you talking to James after the game. Anything going on there?" His words trip over each other as they speed from his mouth. His acorn eyes take root on mine.

"No, nothing is ever going on in my love life, Eric. You know that." James is one of the most attractive guys in our school, and we have Futures class together. But I'm more interested in the consequences of restoring extinct species than in James. Futures is my favorite class because every class is about looking at decisions and identifying all possible consequences. By the end of the class, the media wall is always packed with branches of consequences of consequences of consequences. Mr. Carrillo always says, the problem with the previous centuries is that they always made decisions by looking at their present needs or desires and at the past, bound by a fear of repeating history. They never considered the distant future when making decisions, otherwise the arctic poles would still exist and oceans would not have swallowed so much of the land, and our species would not be suffering extinction like the animals before us.

I peer out the car window, admiring the deciduous trees lining our block. Eric has always been there for me, so I guess it's natural he would be concerned with my love life—or lack thereof.

The car turns a corner bringing a park into view. *The* park. The one where Fiducia died. I've avoided it the last five years and usually take the longer route to school, but today I let Eric take me. I want to scream at him for driving this way. Instead, I plunge down the words with a deep cough—he knew her, too, and it wouldn't be fair of me to scream.

"Are you okay?" Eric's words poke at me, but my mind is on allagine, the genetic disorder that killed Fiducia. I hope to discover a cure for it when I start my apprenticeship.

"Fine."

We finally turn the block, erasing the park from my view, but a part of my mind is still tethered to it. The watchtower comes into view. It's the tallest building, taller even than the wall that surrounds our genus, Genus Gaudiam. We are one of twelve left and protected by walls and translucent shields, though we are connected by technology. Our ancestors would have called this a "city," but it's been a long time since we used that term. Our genus is located in what used to be called Arlington, Texas. We live around thirty minutes from a large, barren ocean—devoid of life—I've never seen. I've always been curious about what life is like beyond our genus wall. Too bad I'll never get the chance, since the only people with access to the watchtowers are students whose career assessment deemed them watchguards.

My conversation with James comes back to me and I remember something that will make Eric laugh. "Oh, James did say something funny, though. He said, 'Tell your boyfriend to call me.'" I pull my eyes from the window, directing my attention to Eric. "And I told him I didn't have a boyfriend, but apparently he thought you and I were together."

"Why would he want me to call him?"

"I can't believe *that's* what you focus on. I don't know why. Maybe to share clothing tips?" I return my gaze outside the window.

"I don't need advice on what to wear."

The rest of the ride to school is smothered in awkward silence. Too silent for his car, apparently, which offers to play music for us.

"Not now . . . thanks, Genia!" Eric tells his car.

My eyes flick to Eric, and I'm sure they're wide as saucers. "Genia? When did you change your car's name? And to my full name?"

"Last week. I thought it would be a cool name for her." He shifts in his seat and sends his glance away from me.

I razz him the rest of the way to school about using my real name. He shrugs off my comments.

· · • ● • · ·

When we arrive on campus, the usual hustle and bustle of classmates has trickled down to a few passersby. I gaze at the digital display on my forearm to check the time. We're late.

Each career prep school is in a different building of what used to be the University of Texas Arlington, but since universities no longer exist, this is where we spend our five years of school prior to our five-year apprenticeships. The School of Cognition is a three-story building on the south end of campus. Eric's class is on the third floor, so he takes the outdoor tube. My class is on the first floor. It's weird to think this will be the last time I'm walking through these doors. It feels like I've been walking through them forever.

Everyone in Genus Guadiam starts school after they've turned eleven years of age, because that is when children stop dying from allagine. I guess the Genus Council figures they shouldn't waste an education on a child who might die. Instead, parents have to teach their children reading, writing, and basic math in preparation to take the career assessment. We take the assessment a few months before we start school, to determine which career we will have as adults. Then we're assigned to a school with a specific curriculum that prepares us for our apprenticeships—and today is the day that matters most.

I walk down the expansive hallway. Most doors are closed, but the door to Calculus class is still open and Mrs. Wiler is at the front of the classroom teaching. I tiptoe through the door, hoping she won't say anything, but the rickety-rackety-clackety of my shoes yanks my classmates' attention toward me—eyes prickling my skin as I make my way to my seat. I plop myself down, the lumbar of the seat adjusts to my body, and the desk swings into position in front of me.

"Glad you could join us, Nia," Mrs. Wiler says, her voice thick with sarcasm. Calculus is not my favorite topic. I think it's because the teacher has had it in for me all year. I can get by, but only with Alex's help. I'm so glad he's in my class.

"Glad I could be here." I give her a just-leave-me-alone smile. She doesn't seem too enthused by my response, but it's enough to appease her, so she continues her lesson.

Sabrina leans over the moment Mrs. Wiler turns away. "Great game last night." Sabrina's soft voice surfs the air like cumulus clouds on a calm day. She's one of the brightest students in class, and I picture her on the Genus Council one day. She's not a hologram either, which is nice. We attend classes with students in other genuses, though not in person. Instead, 4D holographic forms appear in their stead here, and I appear the same to them there. We can see, touch, hear, and smell the students even though they aren't here. Still. You can tell the difference.

"Thanks," I say.

A hand touches my left shoulder from behind. "Alex wants you to check your messages," whispers Robert, a hologram from Genus Amatista, which is on the other side of Domus and used to be called Canada. I open my messages on the screen on my desk—or dreen, as we like to call it—being watchful of the teacher. I'm greeted by Alex's avatar holding balloons and throwing confetti that forms a message. It's a group message to Eric, Casey, and I. In tall black serif letters it reads:

It was great being teammates. Let's all go to the promotion party together after apprenticeship selection.

"Alex, what would you say is the answer to this problem?" Mrs. Wiler inquires, pointing to the calculation on the media wall. I wonder if she knows Alex sent a message out—she's freaky that way. Alex scribbles on his dreen, sending the equation and answer to the media wall for all to see. He figures out the problems in seconds, which is why I'm glad he's in my class. Two thumbs up appear on my dreen from Casey and Eric. I add my own.

"Correct," she says, disappointment dribbling from her mouth. She didn't get to rebuke him for not paying attention. "Now prepare for positioning." Her fingers dance along the digital display on the media wall, maneuvering our desks. My seat adjusts, allowing the footrest to appear and protect my feet from dragging. The desks move into position in an orchestrated fashion. In my mind, the desks perform Tchaikovsky's Swan Lake, my toes tapping to music only I hear.

Once in formation, our four desks—Sabrina, Karl, Esther, and I— form one large screen that displays the first puzzle.

Two desks are at a common point at time t=0, the first desk begins moving along a straight line at the rate of 240 feet per minute. Two minutes later, the second desk starts moving in a direction perpendicular to that of the first, at a rate of 300 feet per minute. How fast is the distance between them changing when the first desk has traveled 720 feet?

I giggle inwardly at the thought of driving my desk three hundred feet per minute. There were a few class sessions in which Mrs. Wiler unlocked the controls that allow us to drive our own desks, but after some of my classmates decided to turn the opportunity into bumper desks, we lost that privilege.

· · • ● • · ·

I head over to our regular lunch table in the quad, where students from each school eat. Metal tables are scattered throughout the lunch area, reflecting the sunlight, resembling stars strewn across a sable sky. The Soshes stick to the grassy area closest to their school. And the Physos hang out near the pool, which belongs to the School of Physicality. Affects are the only group not here, since they're transported—somehow—to Genus Voluptas to begin their apprenticeships in the arts immediately upon receiving their placement. I don't get why they need their own genus. There isn't much mingling with the students in the other schools. I walk toward the Cog area, smack in the center of the quad. I think it gives the best visual of everyone else around us. Invisible veggie-scented clouds excite my stomach on my way there.

In the distance, Casey is pressing her menu options—like some delicate flower—from the box hovering over the table. The box lists a menu on all four sides so students from each side of the table can order at once. I'm blinded for a moment by a glimmer from the translucent dome shield that protects our genus from genetically-modified organisms like plant seeds, harnesses the sun's energy to power our genus, and cleans the air. There is one company that controls the shield—Sustenance. I'm guessing that's where Eric will work, since the career he's been preparing for is Energy Administrator. I scored on the career assessment as a Geneticist, so wherever I go will be a company that hires geneticists.

Eric and Alex—the dynamic duo—are already taking up one side of the table, so I plunk myself down next to Casey. "What did you order?"

"Okra and fries."

I never did enjoy okra. It's odd to me, a chili wannabe with its tapered and somewhat cylindrical form, except for its slimy texture and lack of spiciness.

I slide through the menu pages trying to figure out what I want to eat. Broccoli? Nope. Not today. After swiping through the pages, I return to page one and select garlic spinach and mashed potatoes. For a second I think I shouldn't have ordered something with garlic since I'm going to be meeting with apprenticeship recruiters. Should I cancel it? No. I like garlic. I'll just have to keep my distance from them.

Casey leans over to me, two inches too close, her chin resting on her palm, and whispers, "Is something going on between you and Eric?" Her eyes drill through mine.

I shift in my seat giving myself those two inches back. "What? No. You know he's my best friend."

"He wasn't eyeing you as a best friend when you walked to the table."

"I'm sure he was ogling someone just past me."

"Who? I only ever see him with you. Is he seeing someone?"

"Not that I know of."

Once the guys are done ordering, the menu box rises, bringing their faces into view. The square outline in the center of the table opens up revealing our food. Eric unsnaps the cover from his plate, unveiling grilled asparagus, roasted tomatoes, and rice pilaf. The smell causes my stomach to rumble.

The serverbot arrives at our table with our glasses of water and garnishes—lemon, cucumber, and strawberry. Most days I choose cucumber, but today I figure I'll live on the wild side and choose strawberry. Sometimes I wish we had something other than water. During the inception of the Domus Council, with the struggle to ensure the survival of our species, one of their first decisions was to eliminate all substances that were detrimental to our health. Anything that could increase the risk of our extinction and leave the world to the Immundus had to go.

·   ·   •   ●   •   ·   ·

"I can't believe today is our last day," Casey says, drawing an okra to her mouth.

"I can't believe it's been five years since I walked onto this campus. It's seems like two lifetimes ago," I say.

"I'm so ready to start my apprenticeship tomorrow," Eric chimes in.

"Not me. Did you know if one genus is short on apprentices for climatology they draw from other genuses?" Alex says.

"No," we all respond in sync.

"My advisor said I have to prepare for the possibility that I might leave."

I glance at Casey and from her reaction, it looks like she's just learning her boyfriend might leave her. I can't believe he's telling her now, in front of Eric and me.

"Are you going to eat that or are you teasing your mouth?" Eric says.

While lost in my thoughts, my loaded fork has been hovering near my mouth. I push the food in and give a cheesy smile.

Alex, noticing Casey's face, changes the topic by recounting his favorite lunch items. We all chime in with the flavors we love, then move on to discussing the worst foods. We joke about the vomit-inducing taste of radishes that refused to relinquish hold of our taste buds, even with the cups of water we chugged down.

Then it happens.

Casey mentions how she loves the way her mom cooks okra, with chopped sweet onion, carrots, garlic, corn, and diced tomato, a parade of color that dazzles the eyes and entertains the stomach. My mom was an excellent cook. She never cooked okra because neither my father nor I would eat it if she did. She tried once. I wasn't allowed to turn food down without trying it at least once. So I did. The moment I placed it in my mouth, its texture and taste grossed me out, causing me to propel it across the table onto my mom's plate. If she came back, I would eat okra for her. I would shove it down my throat if that would make her happy—if that would make her stay.

My heart collapses into my stomach, pulling my mind along, as it attempts to escape from the unwanted reality that hasn't changed: my mom is gone. It's been years, but I can still feel the crispness of the note in my hands. The note that changed my life. My eyes become water-filled balloons ready to burst, so I spin my head toward the farthest building, pretending to be distracted by something in the distance. I cough to keep the rush of tears from breaking through. One escapes, though, and slithers down my cheek. I pretend to scratch my cheek to wipe it away, but the thoughts keep coming, piling one on top of the other, and inevitably I think of my father. He might as well be gone, too. He started disappearing from me when my sister, Faith, died, and then when mom left, he chose to give all his time and energy to work, leaving me to fend for myself.

I feel the gentle placement of a hand on my right shoulder. Eric plants himself between me and Casey. The others are oblivious to the tears I'm holding back, but not Eric. He always seems to know. "Everything okay?"

"Yeah. Why do you ask?" I lean toward him, trying to control the sudden fluttering of my eyelashes.

"Just thought I'd check. You zoned out for a bit."

"Oh, I was just thinking about Apprenticeship Recruitment."

I don't know why I can't tell him—or any of them—the truth and admit I'm not strong, that the girl who sits before them is a façade. That beneath my all-together surface is a marred spirit, beaten into submission by one loss after another. Because I'm just a sixteen-year-old girl who wants her mom and her sister back. A girl that would give anything to have a father actually care for her . . . love her . . . want her . . . the way most fathers do.

"Thinking about whether you'll be placed with your dad? This could be your chance to get to know him, since he's always working. If you work with him, then you'll see him all the time."

"True." He'll be forced to talk to me if I serve as his apprentice. I hope.

The bell rings twice, alerting us that ten minutes remain for lunch. I scarf down my remaining food, say my goodbyes, and begin my trek to history class. I almost make it to my building when news holograms appear throughout the quad. "URGENCY! URGENCY! An Immundus has been sighted at the wall near Genesis. I repeat an Immundus has been sighted at the wall near Genesis. Genesis guards are on high alert. Avoid the Mission District and do not drive along the perimeter road. If you come into contact with an Immundus, initiate your alarm."

I glance at my forearm and rub the raised patch of skin where one of my microchips lies. I wish the guard stations would stop announcing the sightings and scaring everyone. All they do is cry Immundus. Who cares if this other human species is at the wall of our genus? I only want to know if they ever make it in. And the wall surrounding Genus Guadiam is too high and too thick for that to happen. At least that's what I keep telling myself. Plus, why would they bother us? We haven't bothered them.

FOUR

RECRUITMENT

After Futures class, my friends and I march to Bridge, the building where our recruitment interviews will occur. All the students from the School of Cognition have to be at Bridge by 3:30 p.m.; the other schools are scheduled at different times today. I scan the herd of people for Alex, Casey, and Eric, but I don't see them. Maybe they weren't released from their classes yet. This is the first time any of us have been to Bridge, which is around a half-mile walk from our school on campus. It's a long rectangular austere building, ashen in color, with windows forming a seamless line of glass along the side of the building. We arrive at the front of the building, where there are six doors, all locked. And so we wait.

"Nia!" An audible voice, the volume of an alarm, stands out among the plethora of students talking. "Nia!" I can't make out who the voice belongs to. I stand on my tiptoes, peering over the tidal wave of faces. It's times like these I wish I was taller than five foot two.

I ask a girl from my classes, Sabrina, if she can see who's calling me, since her height gives her a better vantage point. She can't see either. The crowd begins to split, like the biblical parting of the Red Sea, as people make way for someone.

Alex's face is visible now. "Casey wanted me to ask you if you and Eric still wanted to go to the Promotion Party since there was an Immundus sighting." His voice is breathy, chest heaving, as though he had just run over here.

"Yeah, I don't let those announcements affect what I do."

"I do. I generally go home and lift weights on these days. I want to be prepared if one of those savages ever makes it past the wall."

"Are you saying you guys don't want to go?

"No. We'll all ride together in my car." He rubs his hand through the top of his thick black hair. "Just hang out here after the selections."

An announcement comes through the speakers hovering overhead, informing us to line up in front of the door corresponding to the first letter of our last name. I hadn't noticed before but above each door are letters. The door closest to the left, where I'm standing, is A to E. Since my last name is Luna, and Alex's last name is Sommerfield, we have to line up under different doors. As we split, he says, "I'll flash you when I'm done."

Once in line, a pair of hands come across my face, covering my eyes. "Guess who."

"Eric." He's the only person who has ever covered my eyes. I knew he was bound to come in this line since his last name is Marcello.

"I was worried I wasn't going to be able to find you," he says, combing his fingers through his thick light brown hair.

"Why would that worry you?"

"Because I don't want to get stuck sitting next to someone I don't know."

"So true." I nod my head in agreement.

The doors open and we walk in. There are three long curved rows of stadium seats that belong to each door. Eric and I are assigned to sit in the front row facing the center. Across the room is a mirror set of rows, which also face the center of the room, so I can see Alex and Casey. Casey is in the front row facing us, Alex in the second. To my right are the six doors we came through. The singular adornments in the room are old crystal chandeliers, each with six tiers, providing illumination.

The flood of voices in the room grates my ears. We sit, waiting for instructions. Eric's hands are wrestling.

"Nervous about the place you'll get into?"

"No, I'm excited."

Sound is vacuumed out of the space when a man and a woman enter and walk to the center of the room.

"Welcome to Apprenticeship Recruitment." The woman's voice high-pitched and airy. "I am Genevieve McArthur." She looks young for being an administrator, with her long flowing auburn curls and pink lips against her porcelain skin.

"And I am Mateo Garcia," the man says, poised, his right hand clutched at his chest while his left arm is hidden behind him.

"We are here to facilitate the interview process," Ms. McArthur proclaims, maintaining her whimsical disposition. "There are twenty-eight interview rooms in this building labeled with numbers. In just a moment, Mateo and I will begin calling out names. When we call your name, you will come to collect your card. Your card has a schedule that lists the interview times, rooms, and employer names. It will also tell you which of the following doors you will walk through." Ms. McArthur points to three doors along the curved wall on my left. She continues, "Most of you will visit with at least three employers. Once you have met with your final employer, you will go to Destination Hall, which is analogous to this room, except on the other side of the building. Take a gander at your seat number, and please sit in the same letter row in that room as you are now. Further instructions will be given in that room before you leave." The mass of bodies turns to identify their numbers on the backrests of their seats.

Mr. Garcia clears his throat, and he and Ms. McArthur take turns calling names. They aren't calling us in alphabetical order, and I begin to question why they had us sit in alphabetically-ordered rows in the first place. Alex is called. For Casey's sake, I hope he doesn't get assigned to a company in another genus. Casey follows a few names later.

After almost thirty minutes of waiting, my name is called. Eric squeezes my hand, and I squeeze back before making my way down. I know he's also hoping that I get an apprenticeship with my father. From a distance, Ms. McArthur appeared young, but when I accept my card from her, I notice her face is packed with makeup, her neck riddled with wrinkles, and her scent carrying a hint of baby powder. I'm momentarily distracted by this realization, but then I glance down at my card.

Door One
You have ten minutes to spend with each
employer in the order listed below.
When time is up, move on to the next employer.
Room 1: GenTech
Room 3: Synthesis
Room 5: Codex
Room 7: Genesis

Ten minutes? How are they going to make a decision about me in ten minutes? Well, at least they made this easy enough to understand. My last interview is with Genesis, where my father works. I wonder if he's there in room seven right now.

The door to room one is open, so I walk right in. Three recruiters, a scarecrow-looking woman sandwiched between two men, all in white lab coats, are seated at a table facing me. I imagine they either came from work, are heading to work, or they're working a long shift and this is just a break in the middle of their day.

One of the men directs me to take a seat. He points to the chair right across from them. I feel my face become flush. I didn't think of it before, but I consider what will happen if no employer selects me. I've never heard of a student not getting an apprenticeship, but then again I never asked. I take my seat and shove a smile to the front of my face, determined to make them like me, or at least think me worthy of selection.

"We know you've received high scores in your classes and can do the work. We are seeking someone who will be a good fit with those of us who work at GenTech," the woman explains. "So we want to know about you as a person. Tell us about yourself."

My muscles choke my spine. Tell them about me? I thought for sure they would ask questions about what I learned. I'm ready for those. I'm not prepared to tell them about me. What am I supposed to say? I feel a lump begin to choke off the air to my throat. Sweat begins to percolate to the surface of my palms. I place my hands on my lap, pushing the sweat into my pants and hoping no one notices. I can't tell them about me. I don't even tell my friends about me.

They sit there, with their eyes staring me down, eager to hear a response so that they can cast out the next question to reel in their candidate.

"Wow. Where to begin?" I respond with a voice an octave higher than I expected and with an intense emphasis on eye contact to create the illusion of truthfulness. I deluge them with pretenses of a cheerful life in which my father and I eat breakfast and dinner together, which he makes for me; have long talks about my future and how proud he is that I'm following his career path; and laugh together over shows that we both find interesting. I practically vomit listening to the acrid-tasting words. I share lies about our father-daughter escapades to places like Rascals. Then I bring my mom up the way that hurts the least. I tell them she's dead. It's easier than telling them she left. But the moment I mention my mom, the scarecrow woman begins jotting something on her e-pad. Should I not have said that? Does she know my parents? Maybe she's writing down that I'm a liar because she knows my mom left, or that I'm sharing way too much information about my personal life. Ugh! Why didn't anyone prepare me for this? If my father actually talked to me, I could have learned what to expect.

The truths that wiggle free are about Casey, Eric, and Alex. The moment the recruiters say thank you I'm up and out the door to my next stop.

· · • ● • · ·

My last stop is Genesis, and I worry about how to respond to their recruiters, considering one of them might be my father, or at least know of him. My intestines play Twister with my organs, sending spasms along my spine. I open the door. One person is seated in the room—a man, older than my father, with hair the color of festuca grass, but not as wild. The other employers had three recruiters, so I'm puzzled that there's only one person recruiting for Genesis, but relieved it's not my father. I sit down, carrying my toy smile.

"Hello, Genia. I'm Richard Charleston. I work with your father." I'm taken aback by his welcoming behavior and amiable personality. "He has told me great things about you."

He has? What great things have I done? Even if I had done great things, my father doesn't even know me. But I can't say that, so I shove the truth into the black pit of my heart.

"What has he told you?" I ask, entranced by what he might say.

"Well, he told me you play Spero. That's quite an obstacle course, packed with physical and mental challenges." He rubs his nose. "And received high scores in school."

He's lying. My father never asked me about my scores in school, and I doubt he cared enough to call and find out. This man probably got my scores the same way the others did. And he could have watched one of the Spero games. But I don't argue. I just keep my mask on.

"That was nice of him." I try not to let on that I think he's lying.

"Did you know we only meet with legacies?"

"Legacies?"

"We only consider the children of our employees for apprenticeship positions. Right now, there are three students ready for apprenticeships, including you. So the apprenticeship is yours . . . if you want it."

"If I want it? You mean I get a choice?" I gush, my concerns cascading into oblivion.

"Since we have three positions open and three legacies, you are all guaranteed a position." He shifts forward in his seat. "In Destination Hall, you will receive a card that lists the employers who want you to work for them. *We* will be on the card, but in the event another employer's name is on the card, you will have a choice. Not everyone gets a choice, but you and the other legacies might." He pauses for a moment and looks squarely into my eyes. "We hope you choose us. I'm sure you can accomplish great things at Genesis."

I feel a sudden release of tension, like a dam breaking, releasing a fury of water that settles into a placid state. At least one place for sure wants me. Mr. Charleston thanks me for my time, and I practically bounce to Destination Hall in joy, knowing that my father and I could finally get to know one another after all these years of him shutting me out.

· · ● · ·

I enter Destination Hall and take my spot. Alex and Casey are talking, both seated on the other side of the room. My forearm says 4:45 p.m. I'm excited to tell Eric my placement. I sit mute for fifteen minutes until Eric walks in.

It's hard to contain myself. The moment Eric sits down I tell him about Genesis.

Eric smiles, his eyes piercing mine. "That's great!" His eyes don't pull away, though, making me a little uncomfortable.

"What? What is it?"

He slouches in his seat, staring down at his hands, and doesn't respond.

"Did you mess up in your interviews?"

"No."

I let out a deep sigh. "Oh good." I grab his shoulders. "Then spit it out, Eric. There's something you want to say. I know you."

"Us leaving school just hit me . . . . We're going our separate ways. We won't see each other every day anymore," he says, scratching the back of his head.

"We're still going to be friends. I'll just see you after work now! And it's another reason that we have to make the most of our time together at the party tonight . . . . Which reminds me, Alex said for us to wait for him and Casey at the front of the building when we're done here."

A hush falls on the room as Ms. McArthur and Mr. Garcia walk in. Everyone shifts up and forward in unison, including Eric, awaiting the results.

"The Administration here at the School of Cognition is pleased with all the work you have done, and we wish you the best in your next five years of apprenticeship," Mr. Garcia says. Screams of excitement burst from students on Alex's side of the room. "I have but one piece of advice for you before we present your offers." He pauses for a moment, sweeps his eyes around the hall, then says with great conviction, "Rise beyond the spires of greatness, not for you, but for the sustainability of our world and its inhabitants. Live for the future, that Earth and the life herewith may not be forgotten as though we never were, but live that we may be remembered for all you do to ensure the continuation of our species. With your help, the Homo sapiens will not only thrive now, but for years to come. Carpe posterum!"

We all stand at the conclusion of his speech, our arms crossed against our bodies, pounding our palms over the left and right side of our chest simultaneously in ceremonial fervor.

At that moment, Eric whispers, "I'm in love with you." I hear his words, clear as the sound of rain through the prolific sound of pounding chests. I turn to him, his brown eyes radiating that same strangeness, which I now realize is love, piercing my soul, sending my thoughts caverning into confusion and shock.

I don't respond. I can't respond. Why is he trying to change things between us now? We sit down and the drum of palms to chest is dispelled. Eric's eyes burn into my profile, but I dare not peek his way. He doesn't speak—I'm sure because he knows the others will hear.

The gregarious ones in the group give a few celebratory yells, then silence falls.

I glance over at Casey, wondering if she knew. I hear her words. *Is something going on between you and Eric? He wasn't eyeing you as a best friend.* Awkwardness encompasses my body, even as my mind stays stuck in a hurricane of thoughts.

· · ● ● ● · ·

"Nia." Someone from behind taps my shoulder. "He called your name." Victor, from my history class, spoke as soft as a dandelion on a gentle breeze, but louder than a lily.

"Oh!" I jump up, rushing to the center of the room. Mr. Garcia holds my card this time.

"Congratulations! You'll be working with your dad," he says.

"You know where my father works?"

"Yes, it's my job to know," he says. I freeze in my spot, waiting to hear more. Instead, he directs me to exit.

I read the card:

You have been selected to serve your apprenticeship at:

Genesis

3100 Tansomon Rd.

Please arrive promptly at 8 a.m.

FIVE

ANIMAL MUSEUM

I walk around the building to where Alex said to meet him and Casey. I'm the first here, so I wait. The sun is still radiant and high in the sky. Victor comes out, his face sullen.

"What's wrong? Not the apprenticeship you wanted?" I ask.

"I didn't get an apprenticeship for a career," he said, handing me his card.

> Due to your scores, you were not selected for any of the apprenticeship opportunities.
>
> You will report tomorrow to the Job Detail office, where you will be assigned rotating jobs throughout the genus.

"I'm sorry." I hand him back the card. *So that's what happens.* A tinge of guilt sweeps through me for being glad that didn't happen to me.

"Whatever. It doesn't matter," he says and walks away.

I'm relieved when Casey is the first of our Spero team to exit. A gust of wind sweeps through, sending her blondish-brown hair into her mouth. I can't help but giggle at the sight of her first trying to spit her hair out, then pulling it out with her hand. Her skin is fair, compared to my olive tone skin.

"You knew, didn't you?" I say.

"Knew what?"

"That Eric is in love with me."

"I can't believe you didn't notice. You're always together."

"As friends. That's all I see him as. I . . . I'm going to have to talk to him, but I just can't right now. I need to think. I have no idea what to say." I pause. "Can we hang out together? Tell Alex to hang with Eric tonight."

"I wanted to have fun with Alex tonight, too."

"Pleeeease." I reach for Casey's hands. "I will give you ten of my credits. Just think what you can buy with that." My chest tightens.

"Okay. But I want to spend the last thirty minutes with Alex."

"Fine. I'll leave at that time. I just can't face Eric alone right now."

Several students exit the building before Alex comes around the corner, Eric trailing behind him. My hands quiver, and I feel short of breath. I try to discern from their eyes if they were talking about me.

Alex struts toward us. "Hi, beautiful!" he says to Casey, taking her up in his arms and whispering in her ear. It's something Eric might say to me, like this morning when he referred to himself as my knight in shining armor. I always disregarded it as Eric being facetious. *Was he flirting with me?* I feel naive. I glance over at Eric and his eyes catch mine. My heart sinks like a lead coffin thrown into the ocean at the thought of hurting him.

"All right, you two. Let's get going." I grab Casey by the arm and trek to the car, the guys following behind. I can feel the prickle of Eric's eyes invading my head.

Alex's car is at the edge of the parking lot. Few cars remain. We get into Alex's sleek silver Tesla—I'm seated next to Casey.

"You haven't asked me what my card said. Do you wanna know?" Alex comments, then directs his car where to take us.

I can't believe we forgot to ask. Then again, I can't stop Eric's words from wreaking havoc on my mind. My body brims with bubbles of his words—*I'm in love with you.* They inject me with a warmth I haven't felt before, and they worry me, so I shake them off with difficulty.

"Are you staying in our genus?" I ask.

"No."

"No? Where are they sending you?" Eric says.

I can feel Casey's sadness radiating off her and resonating through me, like some heat wave. I can't believe I didn't notice it before. Alex must have whispered that into her ear when he held her.

"Genus Cormeum."

"That's on the west coast, right?" Eric says.

"West coast, but east of Genus Mare, the one with the largest population."

"Why couldn't they pull someone from Genus Mare then?" Casey's voice blasts through the air of the car, trembling with every syllable. Blood rushes her face to the verge of exploding, like some zit that has peaked.

"I don't make the rules, Casey. But you know I'll call you every time I get the chance. And hopefully I'll be able to transfer back here when the apprenticeship is over." He reaches across to Casey, taking her lips in his. The car feels as though the air has been sucked out and Eric's watching me as I suffocate. Eric and I would usually be talking while Casey and Alex make out, but now I can't help but wonder if he wants that of me. My stomach feels queasy and I'm tempted to ask them to drop me off at home, but I have nothing or no one waiting for me there.

I almost wish he hadn't told me. But now everything is different, and I have no idea what I'm supposed to do.

· · • ● • · ·

We arrive at the Animal Museum, which is larger than our entire campus. Once out of the car, Casey quickly pulls me aside to tell me that she was trying to be a friend to me over this, but she can't do it tonight. She doesn't want to waste the time she has left with Alex on their last evening together for years. Flustered, I agree. So I need to get over myself and enjoy the evening.

The Animal Museum is broken up into the different eras that animal species existed—from dinosaurs to dogs. Dogs were the last to go extinct, when I was six years old. The news showed it as it lay there dying, for all to witness. I will never forget its eyes. It was as though they were apologizing for dying, as if it somehow knew it was the last. I could swear I saw tears flowing as it closed its eyes and took its last breath. It was the first time I experienced that deep haunting pain in my chest that ignited tears.

"So what era should we start with?" Alex asked.

"Let's start with the Jurassic extinctions," Casey said.

"That was so long ago. How about the more recent Patronian extinctions?" I interject.

"You and Eric can check out the Patronian, and Case and I will check out the Jurassic," Alex replies.

I shoot a look at Casey, who shrugs her shoulders and eyebrows and walks away arm-in-arm with Alex, leaving me with Eric. I can't believe she's leaving me with Eric.

"You asked me," Eric said.

"What?" I ask, a rush of heat rising to the surface of my skin as I watch Casey traipse toward Triassic Terrace.

"You asked me what was on my mind."

I turn to Eric, avoiding his eyes and picking at my cuticles. "I know. I . . . I wasn't expecting that, though. Honestly, I don't know what I was expecting."

"Can we talk about it?"

"I'm not ready yet. I'm sorry." I pause as guilt takes residence in my stomach. "Can we avoid talking about that tonight and just take in everything here for now?"

He looks down with pensive eyes and sweeps his leg across the floor. Seconds trudge along. "If that's what you want," he replies, eyes burning into mine.

"That's what I want." I nod.

Together, we amble into Patronian Palace, where the last dog, Hope, was on display in 4D holographic form, she was as tall as Eric and half the size of a car. The speakers overhead give a brief lesson.

Cows went extinct in the twenty-fourth century as a result of the constant tampering with their DNA, leaving them unable to reproduce and scientists unable to replicate a fertile cow. Soon new diseases spread, killing off the next most abundantly available source of meat—pigs. The beef industry quickly turned to sheep after that, until the same happened again. So it went with goats, then horses, and then rabbits, before the industry had exhausted all its feasible options and finally turned to dogs, the only other surviving animal protected by many and commonly referred to as man's best friend. But dogs at the time were too small to feed a nation, so they were genetically modified to be larger and meatier to feed the masses that still craved meat. Many wondered if the thirst for meat would lead to cannibalism. This was the impetus for the Genetic Civil War. With our purist ancestors set on keeping genes pure, the purest lands were taken from those who would defile it. These lands became the twelve genuses that make up our nation Domus. Once acquired and made secure by the walls, work began on clearing out impurities and creating the dome, which now shields us from any potential invasion of genetically-modified seeds, which is where the threat began, since all forms of animals consumed the foods that were genetically modified. It wasn't until a century later that the shield was also able to provide energy for our genus.

As we listen to the lesson, we make our way down the hall, watching as the hologram dogs on display became smaller and smaller the farther back in time we walked.

"Can you believe dogs used to be this small?" Eric says.

"Hologram, please tell me what this dog is called."

"This is a Chihuahua, popular in the twentieth century for having appeared in a television commercial. It originated from what was called Mexico."

"Play the commercial," says Eric.

We can't help but laugh when the dog starts talking.

"What does a Chihuahua really sound like?" I ask. A high-pitched bark comes from the Chihuahua hologram. I bend down and rub my hand against the back of the dog. Its fur is soft and smooth. I look up at Eric. "I wonder if this is what it really felt like."

"We'll never know," says Eric.

The dog wags its tail. *"Dogs liked being pet and were known to wag their tails when they were happy or excited."* The hologram chimes in. By this time, many students were gathered around, attracted by the bark.

One of them asks, "Why did all the animals go extinct?"

"The Patronian era was the last mass extinction. Extinction occurred over time through Homo sapiens hunting, poaching, consuming animals, eliminating animal habitats, polluting the environment, feeding animals genetically-modified foods, and conducting tests on and genetically modifying animals at a rate that was not sustainable for repopulation. Their extinction rapidly increased in the twenty-first century when laws protecting endangered animals were voided and hunting was allowed without limitation for the sake of the population's hunger for meat."

Another student adds, "I read that people would kill animals for fun and hang them on their walls as trophies."

"That's not true," I say in disbelief.

"I believe it. They were barbaric times," Eric adds.

"Yes, hunting was not only for food but also considered a sport in which . . ."

An announcement interrupts the hologram, directing us to the Ordovician Oratorium for dancing. On the way there, we pass a family with two young girls, maybe eight years old. I think of Fiducia and my sister, Faith. Neither made it past eleven.

Without permission, the memory drowns out the museum. Fiducia and I were on our way to play at the neighborhood park. I'd lost my sister when I was four, she'd be twenty-two years old now. A year later, Fiducia had become like a sister to me. She was an only child, and we bonded. We were inseparable for nearly five years. Just a few minutes after we entered the park, Fiducia fell to the ground shaking violently. Her eyes scrolled up within their sockets, arms bent, elbows reaching toward the reddish sky, legs curled back and twisted. A deep gurgling sound came from her throat and a high-pitched hiss slithered from her nose. I stood there, in shock. I didn't know what to do, but I started screaming for help almost involuntarily. I watched her skin burst into scales, sprouting as though she was experiencing an extreme case of eczema. Her eyes sunk in, becoming holes of pitch black. Her arms and legs flailed wildly, a fish out of water flapping against the frigid floor. Flecks of color pulsated through her illuminated blood to the surface of her scaly skin. Red. Purple. Green. Yellow. Orange. Black. Alone, and in multiple variations, as though her body was celebrating with a display of fireworks. In concert with the colors, she began screaming— high-pitched and blood curling. I knew that her microchip had already alerted the emergency unit, just as I knew that when they showed up they wouldn't be able to save her from the incurable disorder. I knew that she was just one of many to succumb to allagine. I knew that although I didn't witness my sister die, she went the same way.

· · ● ● ● · ·

I'm pulled from the memory by a call from Casey. Her hologram stands before me. Since I have my calls set to private, I'm the only one who can see her.

"Where are you? Alex and I are already in the oratorium."

"We're on our way." For a moment, I forget about Eric's confession and take his arm, navigating through the crowds forming near the oratorium entrance, until we find Casey and Alex.

The music is magical, mesmerizing my body, sending all worry away. Soon I'm dancing, and I remind myself that tomorrow's my first day of apprenticeship, but tonight—tonight is party time.

SIX

GENESIS

In the morning, I dress in seconds. I envision the office I'll be working in. I've seen the outside of Genesis: it's unique, designed with spiral spires that reach toward the heavens. They look like strands of DNA. The building is made up of sparkling glass and some other stucco-like material, and it outshines the buildings surrounding it, which are boring in design.

I make my way to my father's bedroom door and knock. We rarely talk or even see each other since he works all the time, but today I'm determined to connect with him since we'll be working together.

"John." I can't drum up the gumption to call him father. At least I'm at his door. That should mean something. I hope things will change between us, that things will get better between us, that there will be a father-daughter us. Maybe working together will be the catalyst.

The hologram door disappears.

"Yes, Nia?" The callousness of his tone scratches at my core, like pumice stone rubbed against skin already raw and wracked with pain.

"Apprenticeship assignments were given yesterday and since I'm a legacy I've been assigned to work at Genesis starting today," I say, puffing the words out of my sandy throat. "I thought we could go to the office together."

His eyes widen in astonishment, as if he had no idea. "Well . . . Uh . . ." His words stumble to the floor searching for bearing. "No . . . I'm working late and wouldn't want to keep you later than you need to be there." His stabbing eyes harden. "You know I always work late. Why would you think that today would be any different? Or maybe that's your problem. You weren't thinking." He turns into his room. The door reappears, barricading him from any response I might have given.

My heart is lacerated by his words. Deep down, I hoped he would say yes. I hoped we could drive together. I hoped he would be my father, show me around, and help me get acclimated to Genesis. I thought this could be our chance to bond, but I was wrong. I seem to be wrong a lot of times when it comes to him. I don't know why I even bother. The little courage I mustered to speak to him shrinks into nothingness. My hope burned in the fire of his words, leaving my spirit in ashes.

· · ● ● ● · ·

I finish getting ready and leave for work in my car. The sky is darker than usual; the climatologist programmed an upcoming storm. I smile knowing some day Alex will be controlling the weather in Genus Cormeum. Then my smile fades when I think of Eric and remember that everything is different now. The buildings around Genesis pale in comparison to its grandeur. The streets glisten like diamonds, telling me it rained last night. Jules deposits me on the front steps and takes a parking place.

After walking up a flight of stairs, I arrive at the platform to the front entrance. The door is reflective, so I watch myself get closer and closer and closer. I get to the doors and wait for them to open. Nothing happens. I touch the doors. Nothing happens. For such a modern building, I wouldn't have expected antediluvian doors. I struggle to open one with both hands and squeeze through the opening I was able to create. Immediately, I look up at the unexpected expanse of space above me where there should be floors. I approach an elderly gentleman sitting behind a black desk centered in the foyer. Behind him are drawers and cabinets of various sizes. I tell him I'm a new apprentice.

From my conversation with Richard from Apprenticeship Recruitment, I know that there are two other apprentices, but I don't see them. Did they decline the offer because other employers accepted them? Perhaps they arrived already and were escorted to their jobs. I hear a noise from behind me and turn around. It's another apprentice. I recognize her from school; she hung out with Sabrina during lunch, and we all had math together. She's even tinier in stature than I am, which contrasts her more to Sabrina's height. She struggles to get the door open, too. I glance at the elderly man, who's watching the girl as though her struggle serves as entertainment. I turn back to the door. The girl is now standing inside.

"Was that door as hard for you?" she asks half-panting, shaking out her arms. "I almost feel like that was a test. If you can get through the doors of Genesis, then you can work for Genesis." She raises her head and arms toward the ceiling, her eyes glimmering.

"Yeah, it was hard for me, too."

"My name's Kelly," she announces, extending her palm toward me.

"I'm Nia." I place my palm to hers.

"I know. Sabrina told me about you." How did I fit into their conversations? Sabrina and I share our classes, but not much else. Just then, the elderly man directs us to stand on the lighted triangle in the back corner of the room and face the back wall. Although it's a rather odd request, we comply. Walking toward the diamond, I catch a glimpse of his wheelchair—clear like glass, even the rollers.

An octagonal section of the floor ascends before us—a door opens. A tall, staunch man welcomes us and invites us into the elevator. Celestial, I think to myself, in awe that the elevator appeared from below. I should have expected it since there are no floors above us. Eight large buttons with pictures instead of floor numbers flank the door. Studying the images closer, the pictures are mainly animals— lion, ostrich, dolphin, mole, kangaroo with a joey in its pouch, and butterfly—but with a plant and door button, too. The elevator man presses lion, and we drop for what feels like several floors. The door opens to a girl, not much older than myself, sitting at a desk. She leads us to an office where the third apprentice, a boy named Mario, is already seated.

We three sit wordless. After a few minutes, a woman walks in and explains a dreary list of rules and responsibilities before asking us to sign a stack of apprenticeship papers. My hand cramps halfway through signing. I understand that the paperwork is important, but I just want to get to work. Before we leave, we place our hands on a pad that feeds data into our microchips, allowing us appropriate access.

Once finished, we're sent back to the elevator, back to the tall staunch man. He presses the kangaroo and joey button. I analyze the pictures on the buttons trying to decipher their meanings. The lion opened to the floor where we had to go through all the steps to become an apprentice, so I'm guessing that was administration. Lions were known to be the king of the jungle, so that's fitting for the leaders of the organization. But a kangaroo with a baby in its pouch is more confusing. What could that mean?

"Where does that button take us?" I look up at the elevator man, my head nearly touching my back.

"To the floor with all the apprentice projects," he says, his iron lips forming a rail across his face, his bowling-ball hands clasped in front.

I glance over at the button again, then at Kelly and Mario. "So I guess we're the joeys."

"It would seem that way," the elevator man responded.

· · • ● • · ·

The elevator door opens to a science lab, large and beautiful. We step out. Each wall is a media screen. One wall shows a beach landscape with trees and flora on the sides, as if viewing the beach from a forest. The water is cerulean blue and the sound of waves brushing against the shore resonates throughout the room. The other walls display a forest, with the sounds of birds and animals. There are no forests in Genus Guadiam, let alone animals, and I've never been to the ocean, so the room is surreal.

Richard from Apprenticeship Recruitment walks toward us.

"Thank you, Henry." He waves to the elevator man. "Welcome legacies," he says, his arms open wide. "This is the laboratory in which you will spend the next five years conducting research with the mentor you are assigned."

Two men and a woman approach as he speaks. My stomach begins to tingle in anticipation.

"This is Dr. Gustaf, Dr. Matus, and Dr. Richter," he says, pointing to each one.

Dr. Gustaf is a tall, lanky man with light olive skin whose baby face makes him approachable. Dr. Matus is about my height, with long, wavy chestnut hair like my mom, and a smile that illuminates the room like a supernova. Dr. Richter reminds me of a military officer with his buzzed haircut, austere expression, and muscular build bulging through his lab coat. He is a bit scary; I hope he doesn't serve as my mentor. I prefer Dr. Gustaf or Dr. Matus, who seem much more friendly.

Richard proceeds to tell us the scientists' backgrounds, giving us a sense of their research focus, then assigns us to our mentor. Mario is assigned to Dr. Richter, Kelly to Dr. Gustaf, and I'm given Dr. Matus. I follow Dr. Matus to her area of the lab. Each area appears to be color-coded. The lab tables in Dr. Matus's section are eucalyptus green. Her team's focus is on fixing the genes that activate allagine. The tables are strewn with equipment and tubes, with even more tubes in the freezer. She introduces me to her team of ten existing researchers, five of whom are also apprentices. Each started within the last four years. The other five are employees who started as apprentices on her project.

"What do you know about allagine?"

"It killed my sister and best friend."

"It has killed many more than that. After years of research, we identified three chromosomes that hold keys to allagine. Chromosome 8, 12, and 22. These are the same chromosomes where the genes for Werner Syndrome, Zellweger syndrome, and DiGeorge syndrome were discovered. Researchers' efforts to eradicate these syndromes caused additional mutations, unknown until the coupling of individuals that held one of each of these syndromes. Over time, these mutations continued. Our job is to identify a way to return the genes to what they should be. We each play a part in this. Your job is to generate in the tube the necessary chemical reactions to crack open the fibroblast cells," Dr. Matus explains. She grabs a tube from one of the other apprentice tables and holds it up. "Derek will provide you with tubes that have already broken the flesh apart in preparation for your task."

A shiver sweeps through my spine knowing that I could be working with the flesh of Fiducia or Faith.

"Let's see how many . . ." Dr. Matus is cut off by a blaring high-pitch sound. Holograms popped up throughout the floor announcing, "Security, please report to level ten. Security, please report to level ten."

Dr. Matus's eyes widened. "I'll be back. Continue your tasks."

"What was that alarm about?" I ask.

"That's the third time we heard it this month. You got me," Derek says. He's seated at the table next to mine. "Every time it goes off, Dr. Matus plays hookie."

· · • ● • · ·

Thirty minutes later, Dr. Matus returns to the lab. Distracted by her entrance, I nearly drop the filled tube and bump into Derek, who approached me.

"It's lunchtime, chickadee," he says, swaying forward and back, his hands in his lab coat pockets.

"How is your first day so far?" Dr. Matus asks.

"I can't complain," I respond.

She glances at Derek and then back to me. "Uh-oh . . . does that mean you want to complain, but you feel like you can't?"

"No, not at all. I enjoy what I'm doing. I can't believe it's already lunchtime." Derek nods at me, a grin sliding across his face, as if he's saying "great recovery."

"Time flows by when you do what you're meant to do. That's the benefit of the career assessments."

"We were just heading to the cafeteria," Derek interjects, pulling at my lab coat and walking away.

All six of us apprentices gather in the elevator. One of the girls standing next to me utters, "What do you think?" Dr. Matus introduced us, but I can't remember her name.

"About what?"

"What do you think about Genesis so far?"

"Well, I love the walls in the lab. It's the closest we'll ever get to the ocean or forests."

"I know, right?"

"What's your name again?" I say, scrunching my eyebrows skyward apologetically.

"I'm Patricia, but everyone calls me Trish. I'm the only second-year apprentice with Dr. Matus."

"And I'm the only first-year, so we have something in common." I smile, not a that's-cool-but-I-couldn't-care-less smile but an I-think-we-can-be-friends smile.

"Yeah. We're the soloists."

She giggles and her cheery disposition makes me comfortable, like a comfy chair I can crash in for a calm night. There's an uneasy silence from the others. One of the guys stares at me, his mouth taking the shape of a smile I'd not seen on anyone before. I'm not sure what to make of it. Should I return the smile, or would he think I'm interested in him? I already have the Eric situation to solve; I don't want to add another to the mix. I decide to slide in a subtle smile—eyebrows excluded—so as to not appear flirtatious. The door opens. I forgot to get a glimpse of the button that was pressed so I could know which floor the food is on, although I assume it's the plant button. Whichever one it is, I'm pretty sure it's above the lab; it felt like we went up in the elevator.

Stepping out of the elevator, I ask Trish, "Do I push the plant to get to this floor?"

"You got it! Plant equals food," she replies, rubbing her tummy.

I pick up on the fact that the elevator man wasn't in the elevator. "What happened to Henry, the elevator man, who brought me and the other new apprentices to the lab?"

"He isn't in there all the time. Only when new apprentices arrive," Derek says, tousling his already messy spiky hair.

The cafeteria is larger than the lab, filled with teal tables and grayish-blue chairs. A line divides the cafeteria starting at the elevator, each side symmetrical. A melody of smells—mushroom, vinegar, cayenne, bell pepper—harmonize into a sweet scent that teases my stomach. I follow the other apprentices, who veer to the left. Trish turns to me. "All the apprentices eat on the left side of the room. Once we graduate from our apprenticeships we move to the right. See." She points to Josh. "There's Josh right there. He's a first-year employee."

I glance over to Josh and spot my father sitting with a group of people. Dr. Matus approaches him, beginning a conversation. *Are they talking about me?* Neither of them glances my way.

"Why are apprentices and employees kept separate?" I ask.

"I don't know. I always thought it was weird myself because we work together side-by-side, so I don't get why we have to eat together yet separately." Her ever-present smile is replaced by a frown that looks out of place on her face. She's obviously weighted by her frustration with the eating arrangements.

Each side has its own buffet to draw from, but I can't help but wonder whether the food is the same. I disregard that thought, content with my options once I catch sight of the cornucopia of delectable dishes. I fill my plate with carrots, salad, and couscous.

The tables are round and each one seats eight. Derek chooses a table near the elevator and we all sit. Silence surrounds us as everyone consumes their entrees. I gather a perfect portion of carrots and couscous, spoon it into my mouth, and slowly chew, savoring every bite. Food at school never tasted this good. I hope Casey, Alex, and Eric are able to revel in food this delicious.

I peer up from my plate several times to observe the others at the table—each focused on the food before them. I can't remember any of their names, except Trish's and Derek's. "I'm sorry, could you tell me your names again? Introductions were so fast earlier, so the only ones I have down are Trish's and Derek's," I say humbly. They respond with their names: Monique, Oscar, and Simon. Derek and Oscar are third-year apprentices. Simon and Monique are fourth-year apprentices.

"So your sister and your best friend died of allagine?" Derek asks. I share my story about Fiducia because she was the one I watched die. The others share their stories, and each one brightens the flame of purpose here at Genesis.

"We can't change the past, but at least we have a chance to change the future," Monique blurts out.

"Like developing diplomatic relations with the Immundus?" Oscar asks.

"No, I was referring to finding a cure so no more children die from allagine," Monique responds.

"Oscar has a point, though." Derek looks around the room and hunches forward. "What if we captured the Immundus to learn more about them?"

Trish's eyes widen in shock. "How is capturing Immundus diplomatic?" Her words propel from her mouth, threaded with disgust.

"Don't act like I'm the only one thinking it," Derek chides.

Monique shakes her head.

"Okay, you two. Let's change this topic. So what are you doing after work, Monique?"

"We need to give our new legacy the Genesis welcome by taking her out for a pint of OJ at Frank's Hotspot after work."

Yeahs ring around the table.

"My friend plays there sometimes," I say.

"He can join us, too," Trish says.

"I'll let him know." I step outside to call Eric.

· · ● ● ● · ·

I scroll my contacts list on my forearm, selecting Eric. His hologram appears before me, it's still on private so only I can see and hear him. "I'm shocked you called. To what do I owe this honor?"

"I'm sorry for . . . yesterday. I'm going to Frank's after work with some apprentices and I wanted to know if you are playing tonight."

"For thirty minutes, right when I get out of work." He says, looking down at his shoes.

"Okay, I want to talk."

"About what?"

"Us." Eric's head whips up at that. "I want to talk in person though, not over the phone," I continue.

He sticks his hands in his pockets. "I'd like that."

"I have to go, but I'll see you tonight."

"Tonight, then."

SEVEN

FRANK'S HOTSPOT

I arrive at Frank's Hotspot, located a few blocks from Genesis. The building is brick red, with an image of flames rising up around the two doors, creating an arch. Oscar and Trish are the first ones here, seated on an antiquated wrought-iron bench in front. When Oscar raises his hand to wave at me, I catch a glimpse of a tattoo on his right arm, on the underside of his bicep. I can't quite make it out. Tattoos are illegal because of the mutagenic chemicals that were put into the inks when fluorescent glow-in-the-dark tats were all the rage—though no one knew they were mutagenic at the time. Now all tattoos are deemed illegal. In a society struggling for survival, I'm mute at the fact that a genetic scientist apprentice has a tattoo. I'm tempted to ask about it, and how and where he got it, but being my first outing with my new friends, I don't want to accidentally create trouble.

When we enter Frank's, music is playing in the background. I search the floor for Eric, but he doesn't appear to be in the room yet. Games are grouped in the center and red and black tables and chairs, with wrought-iron legs like the bench out front, surround the edge. Flame designs consume the inside of the building, even the twisted metal of the chairs make them appear engulfed in flames. How ironic it would be if the restaurant actually went up in flames.

Derek and Monique walk in just as we are seated. Simon isn't able to make it, so now our party is complete. I forgot to ask about the buttons during lunch, so I take the opportunity to ask now.

"What's up with the pictures on the elevator buttons instead of numbers? Where does each one go?"

"You know the plant is the cafeteria," says Trish, reminding me of our conversation earlier.

"I know that one and the lion and the kangaroo," I respond.

"The dolphin is the lab that you get to move up to after serving as an employee for five years," Oscar explains. "The mole takes you to the subway system. That's all I know."

"Subway system?" My brows shoot up with this new knowledge. There was never a mention of a subway system at school. "There's a subway that takes you around town?"

"No, it's the subway that connects the Genesis buildings of each genus," Oscar says.

My mind tries to wrap itself around a way to explain the subway. Why would they need a subway? My eyes cut to Derek, who is staring back at me, a serious look on his face. Does he know?

"So Genesis exists in Genus Voluptas?" I can't think of a reason why the purely-entertainment and artist-oriented genus would need a Genesis.

"I don't know," Oscar says, shrugging his shoulders.

"But you said it connected the genuses. Maybe that's how everyone gets from one to another. But why is it Genesis? Do you know why each building is connected?"

"I was told Genesis is in charge of the evacuation of the genus if the Immundus ever breach our walls," Oscar responds.

Derek's eyes sharply cut to Oscar. Something about this is strange, and I feel the tension skitter across the table. Like we aren't meant to talk about this—except why couldn't we?

"Who told you that?" Monique asks.

"Someone—I don't remember who. I think it was when I first started with Genesis."

Monique nods in acceptance of his response. Derek bows his head and rubs his hand through his sticky strands of hair, his eyes fixed on the table.

He seems like he's holding something back. Something about the train—about the floors? I reevaluate his reaction. Or maybe something about the Immundus evacuation. I don't know what it is, but it's something.

· · ● · ·

We sit in silence for thirty seconds before a miniature waitress hologram appears at the center of the table to take our orders. It immediately alters the mood. Monique and Derek order, reaching their palms toward the hologram so that the two credits can be deducted from each of their microchips for their food and drink. I do the same.

As Oscar begins ordering, I hear Eric's voice announce the next song. I turn toward the stage. He's seated on a stool, playing his classic Fender guitar. I must have missed when he walked in. It's a new song, one I haven't heard him play before. Each pluck of the string is a caress, a slight touch against my soul that sends shivers throughout my body. His voice is tender and passionate, a whisper in my ear. The music fills me, like it has penetrated the very center of my being. I know it sounds dramatic, and I know others might think I'm weird if I told them how music makes me feel. It's why I've never told anyone but Eric. I've always loved his singing, and one day I actually told him how much. He understood it then. He's always understood me. I'd hate to lose that—or him. That's why I know telling him I want to talk tonight was the right thing to do.

I leave the table, approaching Eric just as the song is ending. As I get closer, he spots me. I speed up my steps to get to him before he starts his next song. "I'm ready to talk, whenever you finish your set."

He looks down and thumbs his guitar, adjusting the string tone for the next song. "Okay, I have two more sets." He announces his next song. I'm silenced by his music and return to my table.

· · ● · ·

Trish, peering over my shoulder, says, "Is that your friend?"

"He's cute," chimes Monique. Her finger slides across her lips, like he's some kind of treat.

"So he's a friend from—"

"Monique—leave *her* friend alone. Besides, watching you dig out information on the guy is dull. Let's play Crush," Derek says.

I blink at this statement, but then shrug my shoulders. "Sure. How do you play?"

The rest of the group expresses their disinterest more or less immediately. Derek gives me a quick rundown of the combat simulation game, and then says, "I saw you play Spero. You're pretty good. You always seemed to be the closest to getting out of the maze before your teammates or the other teams, and you seemed to handle the obstacles in the maze quicker than the others. I'm sure a game of Crush is nothing to the hologram fights you experienced in the maze."

I can tell Derek is coaxing my confidence, and although I never played Crush, he reminds me of the fun I had playing Spero, so I agree to play.

Derek and I step into a large square with a perimeter of around forty feet. A digital display appears.

"Weapon, tool, or hands?" Derek asks.

"Tool," I respond.

As he presses the display, two large sticks appear midair. We both grab one. A nervous sensation engulfs my body. Derek is a burly guy who has more muscle than me. Why did I agree to this?

"Come on, little lady," Derek says, instigating a fight. I get a few good hits in, then Derek smacks my rib cage and sweeps my legs from under me, sending me to the ground, and causing me to lose the game. My ego is crushed—it didn't even last a minute. All that time in Spero, and I couldn't even win this game.

"I told you. The goal is to knock your opponent to the ground," Derek says with a smug look plastered on his face.

"Yes. I know," I say, staggering to my seat.

"Just so you know, he's done that to all of us. You can say that was your initiation," Trish says.

"I guess so," I say, holding my ribcage. The adrenaline slinks away alongside my humiliation, revealing the pain that was absent seconds earlier.

The music stops again. I glance over at Eric, who's getting up from his seat, guitar in hand.

"I'm going to talk to Eric for a bit. You guys aren't leaving soon, are you?"

"No, we'll be here. Feel free to bring your *friend* over when you're done with your one-on-one," Monique says.

I ignore her emphasis. "Okay, I'll be back."

Holding my side, I approach Eric. "Let's talk over here." I point to a spot in the corner, farthest away from the occupied seats.

"Sure," he says, leading the way to the table.

"I never asked you where you're serving your apprenticeship." I swipe my bangs to the side, the rhythm of my heart mirroring the beat of a fast-paced techno song.

"Sustenance." He glances over at the table I was at. "So those are the other apprentices?" Eric points with his chin.

"Yeah. Well, the ones on my project team. There are a lot more apprentices in general." I return my gaze to Eric. "I figured you would get into Sustenance. You know, with your celestial voice and great playing, I can't believe the career assessment didn't place you into Genus Voluptas as a musician."

"How could I leave all my family and friends behind?" he says, his face making way for a dimple on his right cheek. A dimple I never noticed before. And then I realize what he just said.

"Are you saying you lied on the career assessments to stay in our genus?" I'm astonished at the thought that he would do that; it never crossed my mind.

"Let's just say I had other plans."

"At eleven?" I remember when all of us eleven year olds were herded to the library to complete the tests that would indicate the focus of our studies and prepare us for our jobs. We were excited to start school, and taking the test was the first step to admission. There were two phases of the test. The first test determined if our strength was cognitive, physical, affective, social, or a mixture of the four. The second phase was a series of assessments based on our result from phase one, to identify the best career fit. Those who score in the cognitive area generally become doctors, accountants, researchers, engineers, or computer analysts. Those with physical strengths tend to become law enforcement, fire fighters, construction workers, and positions in service to the community. Teachers, social workers, and counselors score high on sociability, and kids who score high on affective are sent to Genus Voluptas, which provides entertainment for all other genuses. There, the Affects go through a phase two, to figure out what area they'll specialize in—music, art, drama, dance, voice, or writing. Those who have strengths in all four are taught to become government leaders. Some score a mixture of maybe two or three and they go wherever their highest score is. This is where I fit in. I scored high on cognitive, physical, and affective, with an aptitude toward a geneticist, like my father.

"By the way, are you okay? I saw you get smacked pretty hard. You went down pretty quick, too. "

"Quick is right." My face flushes. "I'm fine, though, aside from my ego being crushed."

"Two days without training, and you're already going soft," he says, raising an eyebrow and smirking.

My whole body smiles at his teasing. It'd only been twenty-four hours of this tension between us, and I already missed the caring voice I have grown accustomed to over the years.

We are interrupted by a serverbot that brings my drink, following the signal of the microchip. I offer a sip to Eric, but he declines, so I suck in the OJ. A piece of pulp plants itself at the base of the straw, so I set the drink down. I want to delay what we're really here to talk about. "Tell me about your interview."

I learn he works in the department that focuses on capturing the sun's rays and directing the energy throughout our genus. He's the only apprentice accepted this year and the other apprentices at his employer don't mingle. As Eric speaks, I recognize how comfortable I'm feeling around him. I feel like myself. I don't think I've felt like that all day.

"And that's everything for now." Eric pauses, looking at me. "So far we talked about everything, it seems, but the topic I thought we were going to be talking about."

I spin the OJ around with my straw, creating a pulp tornado. I always tell Eric to spit out his words, and now it's so hard to disperse mine. I'm afraid of hurting him.

I inhale as though it's my last breath. "Eric, you are my best friend. There's nobody I care about more than you. But I'm not interested in more than friendship. I don't see you that way, and I don't want our relationship to change. I like what it is now."

His eyes glaze over. "Sure, ri-right," he says, choking on his saliva mid-word. "But that doesn't change how I feel about you, Nia."

"I know. Please don't be mad. I'm sorry, Eric."

"Right. Uh, you know, it's getting late. I better go." He grabs his guitar, strangling its neck as he drags it away.

I watch him walk out and I feel a heavy ache spread across my chest, like I've just put on a one-hundred pound vest. I wish I didn't have to hurt him. I wish things wouldn't change.

· · ● ● ● · ·

After a minute, I return to my colleagues, who are sharing theories about the alarm that sounded in Genesis.

"What do you think the alarm means, Nia?" Monique turns, including me in the discussion.

"You probably can guess better than me."

"We want to know what you think," Monique urges me to respond.

"The general population alarms alert us to Immundus sightings, so maybe an Immundus is trying to get into our genus through our building, since we're along the edge of the perimeter, and they are trying to be more subtle about it."

"That's what I said—that I bet they are trying to get in," Trish adds.

"Or trying to get out," Oscar says.

Everyone stares at him. "That would mean they're already in the genus," I say.

"Or in the building."

"Stop trying to scare her, Oscar. It's not funny," Monique reprimands him.

"I'm just throwing out guesses like everyone else."

Derek pulls his fist to his mouth and clears his throat. "Let's play another game. What year do you think we'll find the cure?"

"That's just depressing." Monique throws Derek a get-real look.

As if on cue to break up the gloom that has descended, our food arrives and we all dig in. Eventually, we get onto lighter topics again. Then, after another hour of conversation, sleep beckons me, so I head home. All I can think about on the way home is falling on top of the softly woven blankets of my bed. And when I get there, that's what I do. The day seems a blur.

"Welcome home, John," Sam announces.

Immediately, I'm alert. I've never been up at the same time my father has come home. Maybe I can get his attention by talking about work. I failed this morning, but now I've been there. I jump to my feet, stumbling into the hall near his bedroom door, and catch him just before he enters his room.

"John, what was that alarm that went off today?" I yawn out.

In a stern voice, he responds, "Pay that no mind. We had it covered. Genesis is one of the safest places you could be."

"If it's safe, why was there an alarm?"

"Go to bed, Nia. You shouldn't be up this late."

"I'm not in school anymore."

"You still live in *my* home." His words nail my mouth shut. He continues to his room and I do the same.

I change into my pajamas and then climb back up onto the bed. I lift my knees to my chest and wiggle the sheets out from under me and over my body, creating my nighttime cocoon. I yell out for Sam to shut off the light and admire the shadow of a tree now visible and dancing above me. The rustle of leaves from outside soothe me as I drift to sleep.

· · • ● • · ·

The burning bright of midday lights up the neighborhood. Children run around—laughing, crying, and playing. Some are on swings, others crossing bars through the obstacle course, a few on the grass and in the sand. There are no parents around. I walk toward a crying child, none of the others acknowledge my presence. Sending one knee to the ground, I wipe her tears and lift her chin.

"Why are you crying? Did someone hurt you?" The girl raises her hand to point behind me. I turn. All the other children are flailing wildly, their skin bursting with a rainbow of scales. I want to scream for help, but my voice sinks into my chest. When I return my gaze to the crying child, she is lifted in the arms of a man—my father. "Everything will be all right," he tells her in a comforting voice that I don't recognize anymore. She watches me as she's carried away, disappearing into the blinding sun. The other children are all dead. Looking down, I see the sand is now strangling my waist, then my chest, and now hurdling toward my mouth. A shadow blocks the sun, and a faceless boy grabs my hands and pulls me out. I vomit—excreting scales. The same colorful scales of allagine, but they go pale on the ground and a face begins to form. Lips, cheeks, hair, forehead, nose, eyes. Fiducia.

"Is this what you do to friends?" the faceless boy chides, his words muffled by the thunderous clouds appearing overhead.

"Help me," Fiducia's face says as water drips from above, becoming stronger and stronger.

"I can't. You're dead." The words squeeze out. The water pounds her face, breaking it up into fragments.

"Help me, Nia!" Her mouth gargles the words, until it is no more.

A bolt of lightning strikes me, and the dream spits me back into reality at four in the morning. With my heart still running, I head to the media room.

"Sam—play home movies of Faith."

I watch as video after video shows both my father and mom doting on Faith, who was six years older than me, but even though I first thought she was the girl in my dream—she's not. Watching my family happy, without me, sends a tinge of jealousy surging through my body.

"Play movies that include me and Faith." I lose my breath. Of all the videos for Sam to choose from, she decided to show me crying at the park, in the sandbox, while Faith stood over me wiping my tears, saying, "It's okay, sister. Everything will be all right." She pulled me up, dusted the sand from me, and shot a smile to the camera.

"Pause." I sit, wondering what life would have been like if she hadn't died. I daydream myself into that reality until I fall asleep again.

"Nia! . . . Nia!"

My eyes open to my sister looking at me from the media wall. A comforting hand touches my shoulder.

"I miss them, too." My father sits beside me. I nearly can't believe it and pinch myself to see if I'm still dreaming.

"There isn't a day that goes by that I wish allagine didn't destroy our family. We all find ways to cope. I have found solace in the science of stopping allagine. Your mother prayed to a god she thought could heal our family."

I melt into his caring words. If I knew the image of my sister could soften him, I would have done it sooner.

"Her god couldn't change the past, but I can." He swings his pointer finger between us. "We can. All of us at Genesis can destroy it; stop it from ruining other families."

My head fills with images of the work I performed yesterday. Bubbles of happiness percolate throughout my body, knowing I'm making a difference.

"This is why I no longer want you watching these movies of what we can't change." His eyes speak with sincerity. "Sam—erase all videos with Faith or Fiducia in them."

"What? No? I didn't finish—" I watch Faith's face pixelate and disappear from the screen. The bubbles in my body become boiling anger; my clenched hands force themselves into the sofa.

"Genesis should be the only thing on your mind now." His words are harsh, but his tone still soft. He exits the room.

"Sam—bring back the videos."

"I cannot."

"I know you're able to restore what's deleted."

"That action can only be performed by Mr. Luna. You do not have the necessary permission."

"Uggghhhaaaahhh!" I yell in frustration.

EIGHT

INTERROGATION

"Good morning, Ms. Luna." The elderly man at the front desk of Genesis stretches his arm toward me with something in his hand. "I have your badge for you."

I'm blindsided by the fact he knows my name, considering I didn't tell him. "Good morning," I reply, taking hold of the item. "I don't recall the others wearing badges."

"The new apprentices get badges until the others get familiar with your name," he explains. "I wasn't able to have them for you until all the paperwork was signed and your photo was taken." That's right. The administrator took my photo. She showed it to me after she took it. It wasn't one of my best, but she wouldn't let me retake it. Even now I can hear her words. *Don't be vain. Leave that to those in Genus Voluptas.*

The badge is glass with my holographic face swaying left to right, showing all my profiles. My full name is in bright red against a light gray background; my name appears to lift from the glass. That's how he knows my name.

"How do I put it on?" I ask as I examine the glass, impressed that both sides could serve as the front of the badge.

"Press it to your palm, then stick it anywhere on the front of the jacket," he informs me, as he hands me my very own lab coat. His request sounds odd, but I put on the lab coat and do as he instructs. I begin to place the badge on my coat and it pounds the coat against my chest. Curious as to how the badge adheres, I pull the badge away from my chest and release. The badge sinks back onto my chest. I do this a few more times, trying to figure out how it's adhering.

"Your microchips magnetize it to your body," he explains, no doubt a result of the confusion planted on my face.

That's new. How do you magnetize glass to flesh? And what do the microchips do that make that possible? I still have a lot to learn.

"Thanks!" I say, embarrassed by my dearth of knowledge regarding the microchips in my body since birth. If my mom was around, I'm sure she would have explained their capabilities, aside from allowing access to homes, buildings, and cars. The Domus Council must have told the birthers to place the microchips in us for other reasons. What those reasons are, I don't know. I put that question aside for another day. Today is about curing allagine.

This time, without lighted direction, I go to the spot and wait for the elevator. The elevator begins rising from the ground. I step inside and press the kangaroo and joey button.

· · • ● • · ·

That day and all the other days that follow it for the next month are the same: wake up, go to the lab, go home. I nearly call Eric half those days, but I always stop at the last moment. I want my best friend. I miss him. But he wants something else, and I don't want to hurt him anymore. So, I leave him alone—and so, I'm alone most days. And all days are in the same cycle.

Well, all days, except today, which is exactly one month after the start of my apprenticeship.

This morning, I happened to arrive at the same time as Derek, so we enter the elevator together, along with another man, who's older and much stronger based on the thickness and tightness of his shirt. I hadn't seen him before. After Derek presses our floor, the man presses the ostrich button. A pad extends into the elevator, where the man places his hand and forearm.

"Access granted," the elevator replies.

I look over at Derek, who is unfazed. He's probably seen this before. We arrive at the ostrich floor first, although it feels like it's farther down than our floor. The door opens into another room with a door on the other side. The man steps out and approaches the other door. A laser scans his body as the door to the elevator starts to shut. Just before the doors close, the elevator says, "Malfunction," and the doors stop closing at three-fourths of the way to the center. Then the door to the room opens, and a flash of color dashes by accompanied by a scream. Derek and I look at each other.

"What was that?" I think out loud. The man turns back to us. The elevator door recovers then, closes, and sends us to our floor.

"Did you see that?" I ask Derek.

"Don't speak," he whispers, "not here."

When the doors open to our floor, the alarm is sounding. The same alarm I heard on my first day.

· · • ● • · ·

At my station, a few hours later, Dr. Matus walks me through some procedures I'm not familiar with. In the midst of mixing chemicals in the tube, she says the project team will be gathering for a meeting in the afternoon, then steps away to leave me to my tasks.

After lunch, we follow Dr. Matus toward the beach wall, where she places her hand on a spot on the holographic sand. A doorway appears, leading to a large room with rows of chairs—each row higher than the other. The room seems like it can fit at least one hundred people. I don't understand why we need such a large room for a small group of us. A small room with a table for us to sit around would've been better. I watch my team pass Dr. Matus and scatter up into the rows of seats.

I begin my way up but Dr. Matus shifts toward me, reaching out and grabbing my hand. "Nia, you will need to find the seat you're assigned." She presses a metal box against my forearm. "You should have the information on where to sit now."

I'm reminded of school and how our seating was arranged to accommodate the hologram students, and I quickly realize that scientists will be joining us from other genuses. I glance at my forearm, then make my way up to seat 5D.

I peer across the room, which is filling up with holograms and our own people from Genus Guadiam. The closest person from my team is four rows back and to the left of me. I can't help but wonder if this meeting has to do with what Derek and I saw this morning. We have yet to talk about it. I replay the scream and the painted person running past the door. A hologram appears to my right unexpectedly, sending an audible shriek from my mouth and causing me to jump back into my seat. Dr. Matus approaches me.

"Are you okay?" she asks, concern smeared across her face.

"Yes. I was caught off guard," I say.

"Off guard? That's an interesting expression. Why would you have to be on guard?" she inquires, her eyes drilling mine for an answer. I pull at my cuticles, my heart suffocating at the thought that Derek and I could be in trouble for what we accidentally saw. I have to think fast. I have to give her an answer so she can walk away from me.

"For the Immundus," I respond. "They are the reason we trained every morning to defend ourselves. Which makes we wonder why we no longer train."

"You've learned all the movements you've needed to learn," she says with a healing aloe vera smile, reminding me of the amiable person she is. My anxieties are all in my head.

I know the holograms in school are four-dimensional, so I reach over to touch the hologram next to me to see if I can feel her.

"What was that for?" the hologram asks.

"I wanted to see if I could feel you. I wasn't sure if you were 4D," I say.

"Don't do it again."

"What's your name? Where are you from?" The words rush out.

"Jasmine Gold, from Genus Libertas, in North Domus."

"I didn't know that Genesis existed in other genuses until I started working here." Her golden eyes flicker. Someone squeezes down our row.

"Yes, well, Genesis is in *all* the genuses," she says in a rather uppity manner.

Knowing that Genesis has facilities in each genus shows what a big organization it really is—more than just this building with spires on top. My mind is inundated with questions, which are interrupted by a person at the front of the room. From the slight glimmer on the person's face, I know he's a hologram. Dr. Matus, Dr. Gustaf, and Dr. Richter are seated in a semi-circle behind the speaker along with other scientists, which I assume are holograms, although their glimmer isn't noticeable since they're seated in a shadow.

"Good morning! I am Dr. Gordon Tapia, the allagine project leader for all genuses. We have called this meeting because we need your help," he says, a deep sense of urgency filling his voice.

"Our recent calculations reveal that only one-third of children are not acquiring allagine. In fact, there is a fifteen percent increase in the number of deaths resulting from allagine last year. If this continues, our species could become extinct within this millennium," he says. A sheath of silence blankets the room.

When I entered school at eleven, I was told I was one of the lucky two-thirds of children who survived. I'm sixteen now and can't believe we are already down to one-third of children surviving. This means the daily population counts on the news are a lie. Domus is supposed to host a population just shy of one million, with fifty thousand in Genus Guadiam. My throat becomes a dry wasteland. My father's words take residence in my mind. *Genesis should be the only thing on your mind now. Stop it from ruining other families.*

"It is important this information not be shared with individuals outside our project team. We don't want to incite panic," Dr. Tapia says, examining the matte and glossy faces across the room.

I find his statement odd, considering panic has already begun because of the Immundus sighting alerts. They've become more frequent in the past month and it's causing the community to respond in odd ways—some people are training morning and night, neighborhood guards are posted throughout the genus, and some establishments are closing earlier. But not Genesis. Dr. Tapia goes on to thank us for our efforts and asks us to consider putting in more time so that we can beat this disorder before it's too late for us.

The meeting didn't last long, but while there, everyone hung on every word he spoke, every breath he took, every movement he made. He laid such a heavy burden on us. I remember my dream, in which all the children on the playground were dead. They recycle through my mind, like a train relentlessly barreling down a track. What do their parents tell them when their friends die?

Before leaving, I turn to tell Jasmine it was nice meeting her, but she already disappeared. I gaze across the room. The flickering of fading holograms creates a kaleidoscope of colorful flashes, like the twinkling of stars. It's pretty. I sit for a moment, admiring the scene while others on my team parade down the steps. I'm the last one down.

Just outside the door, a gray-haired but young-looking man, is speaking with Dr. Matus. Derek is by her side.

"Nia." She puts her hand out to stop me from passing her. "This is Mr. Dyer. He would like to speak to you and Derek for a moment."

"About?"

"A problem you may have experienced with an elevator this morning."

"No problem," Derek responds. "We made it to the lab on time. Didn't we, Dr. Matus?"

"Yes, they did." She shoots a concerned look at Mr. Dryer.

"I understand you went to the ostrich floor."

"No. A man who was in the elevator went there. We were headed here," I say.

"Nevertheless, I must take you to administration for further questioning."

"Why can't you ask them here?" Dr. Matus asks, her tone thick with confusion.

"That is beyond your level."

She stabs him with a look of disdain. He walks us through the lab to the elevator. All eyes are on us.

On the administration floor, we're directed to a room at the end of the hall, where the light appears dimmer than the light on the other end. The room is bare, with white walls and a table with chairs in the center.

"What did you hear and see on the ostrich floor?"

"Nothing." The word bursts from Derek's and my mouth simultaneously.

"Don't lie to me." His words were razor sharp, cutting into my conscience. "I have video." The room begins to feel more like a cell.

"Then why are you even asking us?" Derek says. "You saw whatever we saw. Why are you questioning us like this?"

"I want to hear from you what you think you saw and heard."

"I told you. Nothing. I don't know *what* I saw or heard," I say. His eyes are deep and dark, shaped like pumpkin seeds, but with a narrow lid.

"Tell me what you saw *now!*"

"We saw the man. *He* pressed the ostrich button and scanned his hand and arm. *He* got out on the floor. We heard a scream. There was a flash of color. *That's it.* You know what we saw, and it was *nothing,* and we did *nothing.* Why are we here?! Tell us!" Derek explodes before snapping his mouth shut, breathing heavily through his nose.

Sweat forms in a single thin layer on my hands. "Are we in trouble?"

"Depends."

"On what?" Derek asks.

"On whether you're both true—" The media light on Mr. Dyer's temple flashes. "I need to take this call." He steps outside and shuts the glass door. My father's hologram appears. Derek and I watch the interaction. I'm unable to hear the conversation, but I catch one word— Immundus. Mr. Dyer notices we can see him and touches the door, changing it from see-through to white.

"He's getting chewed out. I wonder who that is."

"My father," I admit.

"What floor does he work on?"

"I don't know. I don't know anything."

"Well, he looks like he has more authority than Mr. Dyer. Maybe he'll get us out of here." Derek and I wait impatiently for Mr. Dyer to return.

He walks in, chagrinned, holding the door open. "You're free to go." He sends Derek a devious smirk. "For now."

· · • ● • · ·

On the way back to our station, Trish approaches me.

"What was that all about?" she whispers.

"I'll tell you later," I respond.

At my station, time squeezes by, like when you're trying to get the last of the toothpaste from the bottom of the tube. It's so different from yesterday. One hour left until eight. As much as I love my work, I can't wait to answer Trish's question. I imagine this is what it's like for children eager to open Christmas presents. We don't have "holidays" anymore since they are considered antiquated, but all the classic shows in my Media Studies class had mentions of Christmas and Santa Claus, Easter, and Halloween. The old holiday that fascinates me most, though, has always been Thanksgiving. The idea of families coming together at the dining table for a fancy meal is so interesting. I just don't get how eating is a holiday if people eat every day. What made that day so special?

The figures on my forearm come together to form 8:00 p.m. The other apprentices and I assemble in the elevator. I feel their eyes burrowing into me with questions, but their mouths remain vacant. The temperature rises; my face swells from the heat. The elevator dings.

The group remains silent down the stairs in front of the building before they implode. Their questions come together in a cacophony of words, making nothing but jibberish.

"Not yet," Derek says, in a volume just shy of a yell. He strolls to a well-lit park across the street and we all follow. The park is packed with a variety of trees, plants, and a small pond at the center. Scattered throughout the park are metal picnic tables with benches. I capture a whiff of flowers— Wisteria and the lemon scent of Daphnes. The table and benches are a deep forest green color, camouflaged into the tapestry of the park.

We gather at an available table. It takes no more than a few minutes for Derek to illuminate everyone on what we saw. He also caught the word Immundus in Mr. Dyer's conversation with my dad and made the link that the colorful person running by was an Immundus. But my perspective is different.

"No, it looked like an older person with allagine," I say.

"Adults don't get allagine,"Monique says. "Our science already proved that."

"What if we're wrong? You heard the numbers in that meeting. They might have increased because adults are now acquiring allagine."

"The person was alive though, right?" Trish says.

"I think that's why we heard the scream. The person was confused and scared about what was happening. Maybe they're saving the adults on the ostrich floor."

"Why don't you ask your dad?" Derek adds.

"Is your dad on the ostrich floor?" Oscar asks.

"I told you I don't know anything about my dad's work, Derek."

"When you ask your dad, you'll get some answers."

"Why don't you ask your dad?" I counter. Derek stands, staring at me coldly.

"His dad is dead," Simon chimes in.

My words return and choke me. "I'm sorry. Yeah. Sure. I can ask my father."

· · ● ● ● · ·

During lunch the next day, the aromas in the cafeteria intoxicate me as usual. I search for my father, who I didn't see last night or this morning. This time he makes eye contact and drops a barren smile. Is it an attempt to establish some semblance of family? After all, he's the reason I'm here, legacy and all, and I know he kept me and Derek safe from Mr. Dyer. It's a bit surreal; especially since this is the first time in a long time he's done that, even if it is a feeble attempt. But his smile wasn't always a wasteland. When mom was around, he had the kind of smile that said "home." The kind of smile that wrapped my heart in hugs and kisses. The kind of smile that melted away fears and wiped away tears. I don't remember the reason, the conversation, or when or where it even happened, but I can see it—the memory's so vivid that I feel warm. It nourishes me, if only for a second. As usual, the buffet offers a colorful array of food displayed as pieces of art. I grab a baked potato and load it with tomatoes, broccoli, and chives, with a sprinkle of salt, pepper, and basil. I don't choose anything else because I want to scarf down food and then ask my dad about the ostrich floor. We sit, as always, by the elevator. The silence from the elevator carried over to the table.

"What did your dad say?" Simon asks, slapping his arms down on the table.

I glance around at the group.

"I haven't asked him yet."

"Are you afraid of what the answer might be?" Oscar asks.

"Afraid? Why?" I ask.

"Because regardless of what you both think you saw, whoever that person was is of value to this organization and most likely being researched." The others send their gazes to their plates. "And your father might have something to do with it," Oscar continues.

"What does that mean?"

"Genesis says that we *will* find a cure for allagine," Oscar glances at my father, "no matter what it takes to save our species, they'll do it."

"And that's not right," Derek says, his voice shaking from his upset. "Get answers from your dad, Nia, or I'll get us all answers. That scream . . . there's something wrong here. My dad—never mind."

Monique turns to him with huge eyes. "What can you do, Derek?"

"I don't know, but I won't wait around and let them—" he stops and lowers his voice to barely a whisper, "*torture* living beings, whether they are Sapiens or Immundus. I'll get answers if you don't, Nia."

Derek is beet red and has lost all sense of his earlier cool control and caution. Something has really rattled him. I think about how I've always had the sense that Derek knew something he wasn't sharing.

"Derek, what do you know?"

His eyes cut to mine. "I know we need answers—concrete ones."

I look at him a moment longer. "I'll get them."

I walk away, alone and confused. *Torture?* I need to talk to someone I can trust. Eric immediately comes to mind. It might be selfish, but I think I'll call Eric. I make it to the elevator when I hear my name. I twist back to see my father approaching me.

"How are things going? Are you getting acclimated to your project?" he asks in a pleasant tone. His interest confounds me.

"Great." I stumble over the word. "Thank you for yesterday."

"Gerald can be a bit paranoid. I explained to him that all you want to do is find the cure for the disorder that killed your sister."

I stare at him with curiosity. "What floor do you work on?" I say, my voice somewhat shaky, as I step inside the elevator.

"Does it matter?" he says.

"No, I suppose not. I was just wondering for the day I come to help you with your research—the day I graduate from the joey floor. Like you said. I want to find the cure for the disorder that killed my sister. I'll be here as long as it takes."

He stands silently, but I see the words banging from inside his eyes, eager to come out. The door begins to close, and his hand stretches in, springing the elevator doors open.

"Are you heading back to the lab?" he prods, his head and brow teeter-totter in curiosity.

"Yeah. I already ate and we have a lot of work to do."

"That's my girl," he says, releasing the door.

That's my girl? I haven't heard that since I was young. First, an empty smile and now a *that's my girl*. I can't quite figure out why my father is behaving so peculiarly, but I don't want to think about it right now either.

NINE

CHANGES

I arrive home to find a familiar car parked in front of my house. Eric gets out of his car, as my car, Jules, pulls into the driveway.

I walk toward him. His back is resting against the shaded door panel with hands half in his pockets, legs spread apart. There is something about his stance that makes me want to throw myself into his arms for comfort. I catch his scent—a mix of citrus and other spices—and suddenly, his smell, the smell I always found comforting, is more than that. It's a powerful concoction, igniting my temperature and causing my breath to pick up. *What is happening?*

"Hey," he exclaims with a nervous tremor in his voice. "Thought I'd stop by to see how you were doing," he says, his speech still quavering.

"I'm glad you're here," I respond truthfully, walking toward him. "I'm okay . . . Things have been pretty crazy at work."

"Sorry to hear that." He pauses, peering into my eyes, trying to read me. "Tell me about it." He grabs my left hand and pulls me toward him, his legs now straddling my legs, our bodies almost touching. I know Eric. He must be testing my reaction. I know I should pull away. I know I should make my stance on this clear, but I can't make myself move. Heat radiates from his body, wrapping us in a cocoon of warmth against the slight chill of the night air. A slight breeze brushes wisps of my hair in front of my face, a strand landing delicately on my lips. I hold my breath as his fingers outline my lips, then stroke the strand across my cheek and behind my ear. It feels . . . good, not weird, and suddenly I'm deeply confused. I exhale and push myself back. I've just missed him. Yeah, that's all—I've just missed him.

"Eric . . ."

He looks at me silently. I swallow from the build up of saliva in my mouth. I hope he didn't notice that. And then I have diarrhea of the mouth, blathering about my team, Mr. Dyer, my father, and what Derek and I saw—everything.

"So your friend Derek thinks it was an Immundus."

"Yeah, but it looked like an adult with allagine—with a rainbow of scales."

"Do you think they're capable of killing that person in the name of research?"

"No." I want to tell him the population numbers are dropping and that's why I don't think they would kill the person we saw, but I attempt to at least keep that secret.

"If it was an Immundus, how do you think they captured him? Or her?"

"I don't know." I huff. It seems like I'm saying that a lot. "What about you? How was your day?"

"I saw your father today." He pauses. "And I saw Casey at the commissary last night when I was collecting food."

"Where did you see my father?"

"He came to Sustenance. Saw him in the hall."

"Why would he be there?" I ponder on how what we do at Genesis could have anything to do with Eric's employer.

"Got me. I don't know what he would need to do with the genus's energy supply." His eyebrows crawl to the center of his brow. "Aren't you going to ask about Casey?"

"Yes. How is she? Is she enjoying her apprenticeship?" I ask, but I'm still wondering about my father's role at Genesis.

"Yeah. And Alex likes his job, too."

"It's getting late. I should be getting to sleep," I say.

"Nia, wait!" He catches hold of my left arm, and my skin tingles where he touches me. "Listen to me: I'm still here for you . . . even though you just want to be friends. I get it. I'll adjust. You don't need to . . . to stay away like you've been."

The breath whooshes out of me, and I launch myself at him, clinging to his neck in a fierce hug. His arms immediately wrap around mine, lifting me, mirroring my ferocity.

How I'd missed him. My best friend. My only true friend.

Eric lets go first, gently lowering me. He's proving he can. Now I'm the one to linger before letting go. "Thank you. I . . . needed to hear that."

He nods. I turn back toward my house, and I can feel his eyes following me.

· · ● ● ● · ·

Sam, my house, welcomes me back.

"Is my father here?"

"No. You're father has not been home all day."

Typical.

"The refrigerator is missing lettuce and orange juice. Shall I request some from the commissary?"

Great! My dad must have had the mechbot and refrigerator fixed. "Yes."

I head to the media room, determined to learn more about the Immundus.

"Sam, show me all you can find on Homo immundus."

"There are forty-five news clips of Homo immundus sightings. Would you like me to play one for you?"

"How about text or video from history books?"

"There is no other information on Homo immundus."

Why isn't anything about the Immundus documented? There should be something . . . anything . . . written about the history of the Homo immundus. There isn't even information on the First Species Civil War that the media keeps reminding us of. I continue searching, but find nothing. We must have had the information at some point. Someone removed it, or it's online but hidden from public view. Who's hiding the information? Domus Council?

And then another thought slithers into my head. Could it be Genesis? They have the power and the resources in each genus. Derek and I experienced a glimpse of their treatment before my father intervened, which has me wondering. I didn't think they would kill for the sake of a cure—not when our extinction is becoming more eminent. But then I think about the history of our species. Didn't our ancestors run the animals into extinction knowingly, to meet their needs, without thought of the future? Could Genesis be so determined to cure allagine and save the species that they would kill those with the disorder in the name of research or kill the Immundus to lessen our competition?

Whether it was an adult with allagine or an Immundus, there's more on the ostrich floor than what Genesis is telling anyone.

· · • ● • · ·

That night another nightmare strikes.

This time when I drive up to Genesis, a river of blood flows down the stairs leading to the entrance, a waterfall of death. I wade up the steps to the front door. My entire team is pounding on the glass from the inside, red rain falling from above them. I fall back into the red river in my struggle to open the door, my hands and pants dripping as I get up. Beyond my team is my father, smiling and chuckling. Another pair of hands grab at the door next to mine, and it opens. It's Eric. I look up inside the building where hundreds of people hang from their feet, throats slit, their scaly skin reflecting off the pool of blood below. My team is trapped, frozen in place just inside the doors.

Eric grabs me by the shoulders, shaking me and screaming. "How could you do this? How could you do this, Nia? You're just like your father!"

I turn to see my father with open arms, blood dripping down his face.

"No! I'm not! I'm not!"

I jolt awake, gasping in the air of the real world, thankful for morning.

· · ● · · ·

I arrive at Genesis, half expecting blood to be streaming from the doors and am thankful when it's not.

Two weeks ago I asked the man at the front desk his name and use it now so I don't forget. "Good morning, Clayton!"

Clayton jumps back in his wheelchair. I startled him. I realize then how early it is. 6:05 a.m.

"How are you doing, Ms. Luna?"

"Happy to be alive."

"Aren't we all? Aren't we all?"

I arrive around two hours before my team, but apprentices from other teams are already working. Throughout the two hours, people trickle into the lab. I'm glad I was productive the entire two hours, aside from the occasional glances toward the elevator each time the elevator door *dinged* on our floor. Dr. Matus arrives a quarter before eight o'clock, right before the others arrive. We exchange greetings.

"So, you know my father," I say, adjusting the power of the lenses in my eyes using the display on my forearm.

"Why do you say that?"

"Someone had to tip him off about Mr. Dyer."

She nods briefly. "Yes, we previously worked on the same project."

"What project was that?"

Her head tilts down, her tone stern yet soft spoken as if she doesn't want anyone else to hear. "It's a confidential project that I am not at liberty to discuss."

"How long were you on the project with him?"

"Ten years." At this point, I imagine she's regretting arriving early and working next to me at my table, being barraged by questions.

"Was it your choice to leave the project?" I ask, making note of the activity on the slide.

"Yes . . . it was my choice."

I stop what I'm doing, readjust the focus on the lenses, and turn to her. "So why did you leave?"

"You have a lot of questions," she says, mixing a solution in a nearby beaker. "I shouldn't be surprised, that's why many of us are here. We're inquisitive and want to find answers to many of life's enigmas." She pauses for a moment, scans the room, then whispers. "Just don't allow your quest for answers to override your integrity and moral compass of what's right and wrong." She stands to her feet and moves toward Simon's station.

In a roundabout way, I feel like she answered my question. I think she left because the actions taken on the project were wrong in her eyes.

The dream works its way into my mind again, followed by Derek's theory.

Who would Genesis be more willing to hurt: sick Homo sapiens or Immundus? It's not even a real question—we train for years to know who our enemy is.

So, maybe this all has to do with the Immundus.

Dr. Matus said she was on a project with my father for ten years. Could it be they've been capturing and torturing Immundus for that long? Would my father be involved in something like that? I don't know him well enough to know, but that would explain the screaming and the running on the ostrich floor—wouldn't it? Or is it new, like the alarms that sound throughout the genus?

What if the genus alarms are real, though? What if the Immundus are planning a war we instigated by taking their people captive?

My thoughts run rampant, but one question burns like the sun: what role does my father play in all of this?

· · • ● • · ·

By eight, everyone but Derek has shown up. By break time, he still hasn't arrived. I ask the others if they heard from him last night, but they hadn't. I know the group is slobbering at the opportunity to know the conversation I had with my father at the elevator, since I still haven't said anything.

"Nia." I didn't have to look back to see who called my name. I knew from his voice that my father was behind me. The stares of my other teammates also said as much. "I would like to talk to you for a moment, with Dr. Matus's permission, of course."

"You have it," Dr. Matus replies.

"This way," he says, his arm aimed toward the big meeting room.

"What's going on?" I ask, but he doesn't respond. We enter the large meeting room. He presses a display on the wall inside and the room shrinks, small enough for only us and two chairs.

"I want to know how you're enjoying your project."

"I love it," I say, confused as to why he's asking.

"That's good. But a position opened up on my team, and I want to know if you would like to work with me, instead."

I'm at a loss. I've never heard of an apprentice leaving the joey lab. "But how . . ."

"Yes, apprentices aren't normally able to work with me because of the level of confidentiality, but I convinced my boss that you were ready to learn more about what we do here."

My attention zeroes in on his last words, pushing past my shock. "What makes you say that?"

"I know you're like your mother, overtly curious, and, like me, you have a passion for science. My project can satiate both those appetites. And I think it is likely the best opportunity to be presented to you."

This *is* a huge opportunity, but I'm wary. This is all linked to the ostrich level—I know it. But even if it is Immundus that they're torturing, even if that's wrong, the Domus Council would probably applaud them. And we've been sitting on our theories for an entire day and haven't blabbered to the media. Something isn't adding up.

Then again, why wouldn't I want to work on secret projects? Wouldn't I learn more that way? Wouldn't I get the answers to the questions I was planning to ask my father about this place and his role in it? And part of me still leaps at the chance to work closely with him—to glimpse the man with the smile. I could learn the truth about what Derek and I saw and get to know my father better at the same time.

I open my mouth to accept, but a thought causes me to pause. "Would I still be able to eat lunch with my friends?"

"No. You would be privy to secrets we wouldn't want you sharing with apprentices, so you would eat with the employees."

Without thinking, I utter, "What would stop me from sharing secrets outside of work?"

"Job security. No company will hire someone so willing to reveal company secrets." His sharp words cut into my ego. He has a point.

This path would lead to answers but also to more isolation. I'd be alone again here. And there are so many unanswered questions. So many dark possibilities. Dr. Matus's words ring in my head. *Don't allow your quest for answers to override your integrity and moral compass of what's right and wrong.*

I can't take it.

"Thanks for thinking of me, b—"

"Who else would I be thinking of for this position, Nia? Especially, after the interest you expressed yesterday." My father whips out his question, sending "ut" running back into my mouth and sealing my lips in silence. "Because I've been wanting to work together. Isn't that what you were going to say?"

I narrow my eyes at my father. He knows very well I was about to say "but" not "because." He's pushing me to say yes. I don't know why, but my father needs me to say yes. Instinct takes over. The instinct I developed over the years through the Spero games.

"Yes, of course. That's what I was going to say. When would I start?"

"Tomorrow."

At lunchtime, my friends and I herd into the elevator. Once seated and eating in the cafeteria I break the news of my project change. Monique and Simon throw on their masks of joy but jealousy jets from their eyes like lasers burning into my jaded skull. Oscar and

Trish express sincere sorrow at my premature departure, yet there is a little wariness in Oscar's eyes, as if I've already gone to the other side of the room, as if I'm already part of their secrecy. In the midst of the chaos of everyone's reactions, an announcement is broadcast through the cafeteria.

"May we please have your attention. It is with much sadness that we announce the passing of Derek Monclave, a third-year apprentice—"

My stomach bottoms out, and I break out in chills.

"Did Derek have an illness?" I ask the group. A resounding *no* circles the table.

I feel as if I might throw up.

"—working under the tutelage of Dr. Matus. His father worked here for twenty-five years and passed just three years ago. Derek is survived by his mother, Janet Monclave. As is standard Domus practice, his ashes will be placed in a biodegradable urn and planted beside his father's tree in the park across the street. Let's have a moment of silence now in remembrance of Derek and his contributions to Genesis."

In one swoop, heads bow, except for us first-year apprentices in the room who are unfamiliar with the customs. We bow a second later. In that silence, I replay Derek's words yesterday. I imagine his reaction if they approached him with a new job offer the way my father had with me. I imagine the answers he'd demand that I did not. A deep ache clutches my breast. *Did they kill him?* I sense it's the truth even without any proof.

On its heels, a wave of relief rushes in. This means my father is protecting me—at least he cares enough not to let them kill me. He made sure I said yes. He made sure I didn't reject their offer and end up like Derek. A part of him must care for me.

I realize how deep and turbulent the sea of Genesis is and my inability to safely swim within its waters.

The rest of our lunch conversation is about Derek and what a great colleague he was. I believe everyone at my table is speculating how he died but is too afraid to ask. The conversations at other tables appear to commence as usual as if employees are oblivious to Derek's death, announced not more than five minutes ago.

After lunch we proceed to our lab stations.

"I hear from your father that you're going to be working with him on his project," says Dr. Matus.

"That's what he talked to me about earlier."

She sighs. Not a two-second sigh but a deep belly-filling, ten-second sigh. Her eyes grow glossy, a small bead growing in the corner of her eye. I can't imagine why she would cry over me. She must be crying over Derek.

"It's too bad Derek's father isn't around," she says.

"What difference would Derek's father have made?" I ask.

Her voice drops and she pretends to review my notes. "The same yours did."

She knows then. She just can't say anything.

And for the first time today, I think I've maybe found an ally.

PART TWO

AND THEN THERE WAS LIGHT

TEN

IMMUNDUS

The morning starts off as usual, except that this morning I'm leaving the house with my dad. During the drive to the lab, we don't speak a word. The last time my dad and I had a real conversation was when I was nine. I remember that moment well because I had told him I wanted to be a scientist. His eyes lit with excitement and his mouth brimmed with pride. That left an indelible image on my mind—one that I haven't seen since. Now whenever we speak, it's most often because I'm answering a question or because I need something.

"Before I take you into the lab, I need to go over some logistics with you. You'll be brought up to speed on what we've historically done, what we are doing, and what we plan to do. All the information is confidential with the understanding that you will be taking over my work following my retirement."

"Retirement?" I ask, examining my father's face, wondering why he would even consider retiring at such an early age. Is there something he knows that he isn't telling me? It's not like he ever confides in me, but it wouldn't hurt to ask.

"Yes, retire. I don't plan on doing this work forever and it makes sense that you take on this project that was my mother's, my grandfather's, and my great-grandfather and great-grandmother's. In fact, it's how they met—working on the project. That's why you're so critical to this project and why my bosses are allowing you to start earlier. They recognize your interest in allagine stems not solely from your experience with Fiducia and Faith, but from your genes. You are meant to be on my project." His sales pitch is full of such fervency; I imagine this is how he spoke to his bosses, trying to convince them I could be trusted, resulting in the immediate offer for a switch to his lab. But I still don't know what they are protecting. However, I am growing more and more certain that Derek was right, but still, I want to know for sure what secret they're willing to kill for. The part of me that wants to believe my father questions whether he has any power over the leaders at Genesis or whether he did the minimal he could do to spare me. I don't know much about my father, except for the sincerity of his fervor.

We pull into the driveway, hidden behind the Genesis building, where the parking structure is located. Unlike me, my father has a special parking spot. I watch my father press his palm against Jaden's screen. A flash from Jaden illuminates the garage doors, and they open to what appears to be a large elevator. My father drives in. I don't say a word. I just sit there taking it all in. An elevator for cars . . . how cool is that. But there are no buttons.

"Pay attention. You will need to know this," he says. Jaden lowers the window. "Man is creator of all things," he yells into the speaker located in the elevator.

That is an odd statement considering up to this point we've been the destroyer of all things, including our own species. My mom was religious, but my dad isn't. And she was outspoken about her beliefs. When it came to what she believed in, her fiery nature would always win out against my father—whether she was right or not. My father would most often relent and head off to the bedroom. But they loved each other. How they fell in love I'll never know, but I know that they did. I knew it by the way they held each other and kissed. The way they cared for each other, the way they spoke to each other. But I also know that if she could hear him now, she would have something to say about it.

I feel us being lowered but sitting in the car makes it difficult to gauge how many floors we are passing. The doors open to a small parking lot with ten reserved spaces. We get out of Jaden and she hooks herself to the solar charger. I follow behind my father to a wall on the opposite side of the elevator. Each of the walls are forest green. He places his hand on the wall, and a portion of the wall disintegrates, creating an entryway.

"You first," my dad says, waving me in.

There is a long hallway with a door at the end. The left side of the hallway has what appears to be an animated representation of the evolution of man according to Darwin. The right side of the hallway has the evolution of man according to the bible. If my mom didn't share with me the stories of the bible, I wouldn't have recognized the image of Adam and Eve in the Garden of Eden, Eve with an apple in her hand. The hall reminds me of my father and mother. I touch each wall to see if anything would change. I hear my father chuckle under his breath as he tells me they're media walls. We walk through the door.

Inside is beautiful. The walls, including the ceiling, are synced to make it appear we are underwater in some tropical sea. There is a plethora of sea plants and sea life swimming around, the majority of which I am unable to name. I'm in awe at their beauty. There are four empty lab tables. No one is in yet. My dad walks toward the swaying coral reef and plants his hand on one of the corals. The picture doesn't change, but an entrance appears, opening to an empty room with walls that appear to demonstrate the evolution of the Immundus.

"This is my office," he says.

He then directs me to the lab, each station occupied, save one. This one is reserved for me.

"I have a surprise for you," my dad says, pressing a button on my lab table. A hologram photo of him, me, Faith, and Mom displays. After he deleted all the videos at home, I never thought he would give me something like this.

I step forward to get a closer look. Mom's beautiful—her chestnut hair hugs her face. Faith, with her arm around me. My heart springs to life as if some button was pressed pumping in sweet memories of happier times. Like my mom and dad each holding my hand as we walked through the miniature golf course. My dad, pushing me on the swing and letting me dance on his feet. Faith and I at the park. So good, they almost feel fabricated.

"Thank you!" I say, a single tear swimming down my sunshiny face. This morning has been the most interaction I've had with my dad since I was young. For him to have that picture waiting for me on my desk gives me hope that he can be my dad in the photo. It makes me wonder if he was powerless to do more than save me. If perhaps he's struggling to swim in these waters, too. I push those thoughts out of this happy moment.

"You're welcome. Now we're off to the project you'll be working on."

"I'm not going to work here at this desk?"

"Not today. You're coming with me," he confirms.

"Where?"

"You'll see." He takes on odd container with two small hoses from his pocket, puts it in his nostrils, and presses the base. He hands it to me. "Do what I did. Breathe in deeply at the same time you press the bottom."

"What's this for?"

"It will help you breathe where we're going."

I heave in a breath.

He places his hand on the wall adjacent to his office. An opening emerges, revealing a cream-colored cylindrical elevator. We step into the illuminated tube. The opening seals and a mini digital keyboard displays on the wall. My dad plays a tune that I have a faint memory of hearing as a child.

"That song . . . what is it? It sounds familiar."

"It's a song your mother used to sing to you. I don't know the name."

The memory returns as the song plays again. The first night my mother sang that song to me, I was worried that if I went to sleep I wouldn't wake up. I think I was five or six years old, and I had just learned about allagine. At first she attempted to convince me that allagine would not take me in the middle of the night and that I was too young, but reasoning with me did nothing. She then decided to read to me in an attempt to lull me into dreamland, but that didn't work. I cried for her to stay at my side while I lay in bed, so she did and began to sing. Her voice was sweet and gentle like the hum of a whisper.

Mother's precious darling
Need never fear or dread
For love will always live
Here in your heart and head
Remember, little angel,
That you will find a way
To right wrong in this world
And make a brighter day

My heart is both full and aching. "So . . . the song takes you to a certain floor?"

"This elevator goes to one floor and the way to get to the floor is through this song. You're my legacy, so I wanted to make it something that you would also remember." Slowly, my anger and bitterness melt at the sight of his continued sentimentality. Maybe the father from long ago is hidden inside, revealed only through his passion for work. I'm questioning everything I know about him—and about what he feels about me.

"How long has it been set to that song?"

"The day you started at Genesis." A loud clunking sound resounds within the walls of the elevator. We reach our destination. Wherever we are, it is evident that the elevator is taking us up closer to ground level. We step out into a lambent-lit tunnel with several interesting vehicles I haven't seen before. They have no solar covering, just a bar that goes from the driver side to the passenger side.

We get into one of the cars. My dad presses the on button and grabs the steering wheel. I learned how to manually drive my car in case the system crashed, but I never needed to. The steering wheel of my car is encased in the front panel, ready to come out when called upon.

My father's car begins to rumble, unlike any of the other cars in the genus, which are silent. We head down the tunnel, the car's lights serving to brighten the way. I watch him as he nudges the wheel right and left intermittently, pressing the buttons on the wheel to speed up and slow down. We drive forever until the tunnel begins an incline, leading us right into a metal ceiling, but my father plays the song again on the control panel of the vehicle, dissolving the metal ceiling and allowing us to drive through and out into the air outside the walls of our genus.

· · • ● • · ·

"Wow, I can't believe we're out of the genus. My friends would be so jealous," I say.

"Yes, we are. But you can't tell your friends." He carries a smug look as he maneuvers the vehicle through the terrain. "Aren't you glad you came with me rather than stay in the lab?"

"Yeah! But what are we doing here?" I ask, perplexed. Even as my confusion spreads, I relish the beauty of the luscious mixture of trees, colorful flora, and golden brown rolling hills that abound around me. Beyond the run of trees is a clearing. I turn my head around to observe the massiveness of our genus, its brown rock textured walls blending into nature, although it can't compare with nature, Earth's ultimate artist. In contrast, the walls on the inside of the genus are a dreary gray.

One of the guard posts is located atop the wall over the genus exit. Guard posts are located every ten miles around the wall. I know because I measured the distance one time I took a drive along the perimeter road. The guard posts make Genus Guadiam appear like an old castle from the outside. The genus walls tower above all the buildings except the watchtower.

"We're out here to hunt for Immundus," his response a bit too excited.

"Hunt . . . Immundus . . . Did you just say you *hunt* Immundus?"

"Yes, many of them. Each Immundus gene mutation is at different stages, so the more Immundus we catch or tag, the more information we can obtain to formulate a broader picture of their genetic mapping."

I struggle with the reality of what my father is saying; my thoughts battle for center stage until one comes forth. It was an Immundus that we saw on the ostrich level. Solace slips over me like a warm blanket—at least allagine isn't spreading to adults. But it's soon replaced with disgust. I don't know anything about the Immundus, but they are living beings.

I picture the animals from the museum. I couldn't believe that people really hunted animals, and here I am with my dad, hunting Immundus. Joy slips from my body. I try to understand why he feels the need to do this.

"I don't understand. Is that your project? To map the Immundus gene? I . . . I thought every project at Genesis was focused on curing allagine and saving our species."

"They are—as is this one."

"But what do the Immundus have to do with allagine?" Something tickles in the back of my mind. I remember the Immundus running by the door of the ostrich floor. Their skin. Their skin wasn't just similar to an allagine victim's—it was identical to one.

My mind races, trying to put it all together. Why would they have the same skin? Does allagine originate from the Immundus—do they somehow inadvertently spread the disorder to us? Is that possible?

As I fight to comprehend what fuels my father to hunt down another species, he suddenly breaks my concentration. "Nia, grab the tranquilizer gun."

"What?"

"Grab the tranquilizer gun and load it with the needles in that case," he repeats, pointing to a bluish-black case in the back. The tranquilizer gun is in a slot between us. Two people are in the distance, bending down, unaware of our approach. I open the case and my eyes narrow in on the lemon-colored fluid in the bullet syringe.

"What does it inject them with?" I ask, rolling the bullet syringe between my fingers.

"It's to knock them out so we can take them to the lab."

Take them to the lab? This confirms further that it was an Immundus Derek and I saw awake and running for his life. I know how to load an injector gun from my combat training, but the thought of shooting two innocent Immundus for no reason except who they are makes my stomach churn. We move closer, I hear a melody floating in the wind. It's soft, but it sounds like the song my dad played in the elevator.

"Hear that, Dad?"

"What?"

"The song! The song you played in the elevator. The one Mom used to sing," I say.

"I don't hear anything," he says. Just then the Immundus spring up, somehow alerted to our impending arrival, and begin to run away.

I study the Immundus in awe—this is much different than the blur I saw on the ostrich level. Now, I can see them—and they are not so very different from Sapiens.

"Shoot them . . . shoot them both!"

I picture Eric in the animal museum: *They were barbaric times.* What would he think of me if he knew what I am about to do?

"No," I say under my breath, but I'm able to garner some backbone and repeat it with indignant repulsion. "No . . . I won't do it! This is insanity!"

"Fine. Get over here and grab the wheel."

I almost refuse, but I know refusal would be futile. We switch places, my hands fumbling for the wheel in order to keep the vehicle moving. The car jumps forward, faster than before.

"Don't press the buttons too far down!"

I release the pressure from the buttons and the jeep slows down, but not too much. The Immundus are no match for this speeding vehicle heading for them. The first one trips, becoming easy prey; the tranquilizer hits the right shoulder blade, causing him or her to collapse to the ground. The second shot misses the other Immundus, but the third one lands in the center of its back. A wicked smile is unleashed on my father's face. My head feels like it could float off my body. My stomach is sullen, thrusting up its contents, which my throat kicks back.

"Why do you do this? Why do you hunt them? What is so important about their genes?" Some part of me hopes his answer will give him even the smallest redemption—that even a fraction of good can come from this barbaric practice. Here, outside Genesis, outside the genus, I want an answer.

"Not now, Nia! I'll explain everything when we're back and safely inside. You needed to come today, so I could show administration that you have the backbone for our family's work."

"What is our family's work? What is this? What are we doing?" I shout.

"Nia! Not now, I said. Come over here and help me lift this one into the transporter."

My body goes numb with shock, and I slowly do my father's bidding without even paying attention to the task. I thought I knew what Genesis might be doing—whatever I thought, it was nothing compared to this. I can't understand it.

"Okay. Let's get out of here, we got what we wanted," he bellows, stepping into the vehicle.

"What *you* wanted. I don't want any part of whatever this is!"

I sit, muted, during the return to our genus. I make the connection that the guards know my dad has been collecting Immundus, yet they haven't done anything about it. The Domus Council governs the guards, so they are aware of the Immundus hunting. It's obvious our government does not care. The public is terrified and becoming more aggressive these days toward the Immundus, and the government knows that we are the hunters and they are our prey. So why is this being kept secret from the public? I can't make sense of any of this and now I have more questions than I started with.

Once we get close enough, the doors that lead under the genus disappear. We park. My father makes a call and within minutes, two well-built men arrive with gurneys, one for each Immundus. I glance at the door to the tubular elevator and I get out of the vehicle, curious how the guys with the gurneys arrived. I didn't see them come out of it, so maybe there is another door they came through. The lissome bodies of the Immundus are moved from the vehicle to the gurney.

My dad said earlier that there was a decontamination room we go through to keep outside particles from making it into our genus. I search the walls for readers, but I don't see any other potential doors. BOOM! A wall pounds into the ground, separating the garage from the rest of the tunnel.

"Close your eyes for decontamination!" my dad yells. I close them. A radiant light penetrates my eyelids. I squeeze my eyes tighter.

I want to complain that he should have told me to expect this. Instead, I pull the image of the photo on my desk of my mom and him and a different time. After a few seconds, my dad yells *clear*. I open my eyes and blink a few times to regain some semblance of normal vision. The gurney pushers place white sheets over each body. They stand with the gurney near the elevator on a section of what appears to be hardened sand. I hadn't noticed it before since I was enthralled with the vehicle and tunnel. My father approaches, placing his hand on the elevator. A digital display appears, and the elevator stretches wide enough to fit the two gurneys, gurney pushers, my dad, and myself.

· · ● ● ● · ·

Back in his office, I wait for the door to close before I explode.

"What is going on here?! I want an explanation right now! What does the genetic mapping of an Immundus have to do with anything we do here? And why must you hunt them to do it?"

I take a seat and listen to my father explain his actions, his project, our family's project, which dates further back than my great-great-grandparents and both their lines.

My father leans forward, his arms crossed on his desk, and says the most unexpected thing. "Everything begins with our family history."

"Our family history?"

"Yes, our family created the Homo immundus."

"How can *we* have created a new species of man?" I say after my brain processes his words. The continuous stream of new information has me addlebrained.

"Our ancestors created the genetically-modified foods that started the chain reaction that is now the Immundus."

"I still don't understand," I say, frustrated at my lack of perception and the fog of shock that isn't helping matters. "How can that be? And how are the Immundus related to allagine? I figured out that their skin is the same, but I don't understand why. Did the disorder that's killing off our species originate from the Immundus?"

"In a manner of speaking. Let us address this one step at a time. First, Hippocrates, the father of medicine once said, 'Let food be thy medicine.'"

"Yeah . . . and?"

"He forgot to leave out how food could also be our downfall." He pauses to glance at the Immundus on the wall.

"You're not making sense."

"During the twentieth century, scientists began introducing chemicals into food, both to keep insects from eating the food, but also to maximize the money they made by producing bigger and better crops. People consumed the food and all the chemicals." He stands up and walks toward the wall with the picture of Immundus. "When you bring together chemicals in a beaker and place it over a bunsen burner, a chemical reaction occurs."

"Yes, I know."

"Human bodies were like the beaker, loaded with chemicals from the foods they ate. The sun served as the bunsen burner." He lets this sink in a moment, only moving on when understanding dawns on my face. "In the beginning, people's bodies reacted with diseases, skin conditions, and disorders. This was the body's way of managing the genetic changes that were occurring. Some bodies weren't able to adjust to the changes and died from resulting conditions the medical community could not cure. For those who survived, the changes were minimal. The genetic modifications were passed to their offspring who continued the same process of ingesting chemicals through man-made foods. This process of change continued until the first Homo immundus was born. All it took was time."

Time. Warning bells are setting off in my head. I grab for a logical, scientific question.

"How can you know for sure that was the source of the mutation?"

"We've confirmed it through this project. It's not correlation—it's causation. For the world back then, it wasn't until it was too late that they realized the power of the chemicals they were using. Fortunately, purist colonies had already started to protect areas of land from contamination—that later became our genuses."

Causation. But even as my thoughts are flying at light speed toward the answer to the puzzle, one thought bothers me: I can't understand how some of us are still Homo sapiens.

"Why haven't all of us changed?"

"We all carry the gene, but it is only active in some of us. That is why we must figure out how to deactivate it or remove it somehow."

The room is bereft of sound. *Activate.* What activates genes? What activates hormonal changes? *Puberty.*

And suddenly like a light turned on in a room, I understand everything. Allagine isn't a disorder, it's a transformation, an activation. Allagine and Immundus are one in the same. People aren't dying—they are *evolving.* The implications are overwhelming. The world is upside down, but here, right now, I will put my father on trial.

"Why are we hunting Immundus and bringing them here?" I ask, raising my voice, eager to hear the response.

"We are trying to cure them. To fix the problem our ancestors created. The one way we can help them and return them to normal is by capturing them and running tests. But just like the time it took to get them to this point, it is going to take time to see the results of our various tests. We won't be able to see real changes for at least another millennia."

Cure them? But how can you cure evolution?

And then it hits me—if they are transforming, then they aren't dying. Which means they are alive.

"Where are they?" My body surges with the possibility that Faith and Fiducia are alive.

My father doesn't pretend to misunderstand me.

"Here." His face is emotionless.

"Faith is here?" The beating of my heart is now drumming in my ears.

"No, your sister isn't."

I wait for him to respond, but he just sits there, holding her location in the confines of his mouth. "Where is she?"

"Dead."

My heart feels as though it's been dipped in stomache acid. "But—"

"She didn't survive the transformation. A rare few don't."

"Fiducia?"

"Yes, we have her. Alive."

"Fiducia is here . . . in this building?" I say in disbelief. My hands and legs shake at the thought that my friend is so close—is alive.

"Yes."

"Take me to her. Please."

"No . . . not yet. There's work to do first."

"Please. Please take me to her," I scream, my hands choking the arms of the chair.

"If you want to see your friend, you are going to have to follow my rules. You are here because of me. You are *my* legacy and our work must continue, Nia. We owe it to the Immundus and those becoming Immundus. We're the reason they exist. So we must be the reason they can be changed back."

"Why do we have to change them? It seems they can survive the way they are—can't they?" I know so little of them. I wonder if they are more primitive in their cognitive development than we are. Does the transformation harm or stunt their mind? If it did, this would make more sense.

"They are a monstrosity!" he says, his disgust evident in his voice.

"How? Are they harmed by the transformation?"

"No, Nia, don't you understand? They should not *exist* the way they are now and if we allow their kind to persist, there might be greater negative ramifications for our kind as a result." His eyes grow riddled with angst, his body tense, evident by protruding veins, clenched fists, and rigid posture.

"You mean Sapiens becoming extinct."

"We can't leave a mistake left to survive," he says.

I fall into myself, realizing the complexity we face in resolving the Immundus strain. With every new birth, the child incorporates the Immundus gene from the mother and father. So with each new birth, the Immundus gene could become more dominant, which could be why more children are turning. "Curing" ourselves of the gene seems an impossible feat, but it doesn't change the fundamental fact that it is not a disorder that harms them, it is an evolutionary adaptation.

"Aren't they just the next stage of evolution? We have become the Neanderthals; they are the future."

"Never, Nia! You must not give up! We can fix the mistakes we made."

"This is not my doing or yours. Our ancestors are the reason for the existence of the gene."

"We have an obligation to our ancestors who are expecting us to continue this work. And it is our name that we must clear from the history records," he says. I feel sorry for my father then, for caring so much about a reputation that he's become like our ancestors—brutal and callous in his determination toward his goals.

"I searched for information on the history of the Immundus, but I couldn't find any. What history records are you talking about?"

"The Domus Council agreed to have them withheld from public viewing until we can clear our name—but they still exist and are in their possession."

The mention of the council lights my fury. They know the truth about the Immundus but have been weaving tales throughout the genuses to instill fear—to make us afraid of an invisible threat.

"Nia!" My father's voice sounds distant, even though he is seated across the table.

"What?" I ask, still drunk with the influx of knowledge and what it all means.

"Do you have any other questions before I introduce you to the team and show you our work?"

Yes. But I don't think he will give me the answers I need. Instead, I'll find out for myself. "No."

"Do you now understand why you are on my project team?"

I give him what he wants to hear. "We have to correct the genetic modifications caused by our ancestors or else Homo sapiens might become extinct."

"Excellent," his words drizzle out. "You understand."

I do, but I'm not as blindly dedicated to the cause as my father, because I know it's more complicated than that. There might not be anything to correct—Immundus are the next stage of evolution. I also don't know what that means for my species. There is one thing I know for sure. I'll never have the same glee from hunting that my father has. The nausea rises up again. I can't bear the thought of Fiducia locked up somewhere in here.

"Dad." I pause, letting that name sink in for both of us. "I understand, but before we begin our work, I would really like to see Fiducia . . . just see her." I can see he is entirely unmoved. So I say the one thing that might affect him. "I need to see my patient. I need to see what we are correcting, if you want me motivated."

"Fine," he pushes the word out. "I will take you to *see* her."

"Now?"

"If that's what you want."

"That is what I want," I say, for once telling him the entire truth.

· · ● ⬤ ● · ·

I follow behind my father, every part of me rejoicing, knowing I'm about to see Fiducia.

We return to the parking garage, but instead of walking to the large service elevator, we walk to the left side of the garage, in front of some cars. He places his hand on the wall reader and a door appears. We enter a long corridor lined with rooms on both sides. Through the window of three of the rooms, I see several Immundus sharing the space.

"Why are some Immundus in groups and others alone?" I ask.

"The ones in groups are recent captures. We are building another wing of rooms to house them, but until it is complete, they have to share space."

We turn a corner and I spot an elevator in the distance, along the left-side wall.

I find it odd that, considering the number of children who transformed over the years, there are few rooms with single inhabitants. There should be hundreds of single rooms. "You said children die on rare occasions when they transform into Immundus, so where are the live children at? You don't have enough rooms here to house all the children who acquired allagine."

"Well, I wasn't one-hundred percent truthful when I said it was rare that children died. It's rare that they die immediately, while many take weeks to die because their organs reject the changes. Your friend, Fiducia, is one of the lucky ones. She survived and goes by Dasha now," he announces.

The many corridors we've taken remind me of the mazes of Spero, but without the obstacles. We slow to a stop in front of a window just down one of the corridors. Inside, Fiducia is sitting with a book in her hands. The cover is tattered. I remember she liked books. Sometimes she would bring books to read in the park. I try to make out the title of the book she is reading, but she's too far away and her hand is over part of the cover. Her curly black hair rests on her shoulders.

She senses our presence and turns around. Our eyes connect. Her eyes no longer emanate a gentle caring shimmer like they did so long ago. Now they're harsh, lost in a sea of discontent. She inspects me for what seems like a decade. I place my hand up to the window and wave, hoping she will remember me. We both look different. Her skin is now covered in iridescent scales that glimmer quietly in a multitude of color. They're more similar to alligator scales. Her nails are a little curved like claws but not as big as I imagined them. They're the length of mine, just beyond my finger, and they are sharp, but in no means razor sharp. I didn't expect her to look so much like us, wearing a white T-shirt and baggy gray pants. Her eyes are still dark human eyes, though they reflect oddly in the light—the way a dog's or cat's eye would have—an adaptation for better night vision. Her teeth are no different from mine. Her hair is curlier than I remember it, and even though she's sitting, I can tell by her legs she is tall. Unlike me, she didn't stop until she hit at least five eleven.

As my eyes roam her skin, they catch on a long line on her arm. I don't understand what it is at first, then realize her scales are shaved off here—intentionally. It takes a second for me to recall the samples in the lab. Samples that I thought were from deceased victims of allagine. I sway against the door and cling to sharp, irrational hope.

"Father. The samples in the lab. Are they from failed transformations?"

"Yes—" I nearly collapse in relief at the word, my mind already explaining that Fiducia's arm must have been some kind of accident, when I hear my father still speaking, "some are. But most samples are better to use fresh."

My eyes whip to his, cold in their logic, and then to Fiducia's arm.

We aren't just capturing, imprisoning, and falsely spreading fear about the Immundus, we're torturing them. The Immundus aren't the monstrosity—we are.

I grasp the reality that I'm going to be a large disappointment to my father.

"Nia, it's requisite to find the cure. We have no other alternative."

I cannot respond to him now. I cannot tell him any of my ardent resolutions. I cannot tell him that it is better that our kind falls to extinction than treat the Immundus this way. He will not understand. For now, I look into Fiducia's eyes.

Does she blame me for her predicament since she was with me one moment and then here the next? I imagine her asking herself: *Did our friendship and my life mean so little to her that she was willing to give me up to her father?* She knew who my father was before she changed.

Seeing her isn't going to be enough, I need to speak with her.

"Okay. That's it. Time's up," my father proclaims. He starts heading back the way we came.

"Can I talk with her? For just a moment . . . to clear things up?" I sputter.

"There's nothing to clear up. Her gene turned on and yours didn't. Now be a geneticist, be a scientist, and clear your mind for the work ahead."

Yes, the work ahead. On the way back to my father's lab, I don't even realize I'm scanning the walls for potential cameras until halfway. I become increasingly aware that my work and his work might be different.

ELEVEN

TRUST

When I walk into the cafeteria later that day, I see my friends chatting at our regular table. In the food line, I continue to glance over their way, hoping one of them will see me so I can wave at them. But each time I turn their way, no one looks. It's as if I was never at their table—like for them I never existed. I don't think they notice when I sit with my dad either. I sink into thoughts of Fiducia and the other Immundus. A nudge returns me to alertness, and I see Dr. Matus looking at me expectantly. The food on my plate is already half eaten, and I don't even recall eating it.

"How are you enjoying your first day with your father?" Dr. Matus repeats.

"It's great!" I say, taking every ounce of energy I contain to get those words to clear my mouth. By her facial expression, I gather she doesn't buy it. I need to become a better liar.

"She went out with me today like you used to," my father chimes in, boasting, as if it was something to be proud of.

Her own eyes widen. "Well, then. I know someone's eyes have been opened."

"Yes, they have," I say, biting into a cinnamon-glazed carrot stick.

"Well, I hope you know you are breaking barriers. You are the first apprentice to ever be allowed on a project like your father's and the first to eat on our side. You're turning out to be quite the rebel."

"Rebel? Now let's not exaggerate, Maria," says my dad.

"I'm not a rebel," I say, shaking my head in disagreement.

"I'm not saying it in a bad way. I think it's time for change." She winks at me and struts off. I catch my father gazing at her, not that he's trying to hide it.

"Did you and Dr. Matus ever have a relationship?" I ask.

My father's head whips toward me until his eyes convene at mine. His face flushes. "What makes you say that?"

"The way you were looking at her right now."

"No." His shoulders shrug forward. He focuses his attention on his plate, moving his food side-to-side like a pendulum. "It would have never worked out. We have different values," his discontented tone reveals a hidden desire for a relationship.

So do we. Earlier, I thought Dr. Matus might be an ally for me here, but I'm still not sure if I can confide in her. I don't know her—or this place—well enough. I know Genesis will kill to protect this secret, and I don't know this playing field well yet. In an instant, I feel like I'm back on the Spero field, having just entered the maze.

The thought reminds me of Eric, and I come to a decision. But I'll need my car. From my forearm, I request Jules to pick me up after work.

When the clock shifts to 8 p.m. I rush to the front of the building where I asked Jules to meet me. The moment I enter the car, I call Eric.

"Nia?"

"Hi, Eric, I . . . I hope it's okay I called. I just had to today."

"Of course it's okay. What's wrong?"

I've always known how well Eric knew me. I don't think I understood how rare that gift was until now. "Can you meet me somewhere to talk?"

"Right now?" His voice seemed eager.

"If it's not too late for you." A tinge of guilt brushes across my heart. I know that he'll see me regardless of the time.

"No, it's not. Where do you want to meet?"

Places dot my mind. One place in particular captures my attention. "Meet me at the park near our homes. Be there in five minutes."

"I'll walk over right now."

· · • ● • · ·

Eric sits on a swing, shifting it side to side, his arms wrapped around the chains. The surrounding lights illuminate his face. A shadow dances along the slide from a flickering post. The wind caresses the trees, sending shivers through its leaves.

"I was shocked you suggested coming here . . . especially after getting mad at me for passing by here in the past."

"That's what I want to talk to you about," I admit in a rushed tone. I shouldn't tell him, but I'm going to anyway. He's my best friend, and this secret is too much for me to bear alone. I need someone who I know I can trust.

"About you getting mad at me?"

"No, that I'm not haunted by this park anymore."

"What changed?"

I sit down in the swing beside him. "I have a secret I want to share, but you have to promise not to reveal it to anyone," I say with a slight crackle in my throat.

He turns the swing toward me. "Of course. You can trust me. I hope you know that."

I peer into his eyes, hoping we can somehow seal this pact between us. I gulp down a breath. "Fiducia is not dead."

He stares, his mind brandishing wrinkles upon his brow. "If she's not dead, where is she?"

"Locked up in Genesis—with the other Immundus."

"Other Immundus?"

"There is no such thing as allagine. It's a lie. The children are turning into Immundus." Even though I speak the words, it's still hard for me to accept and I worry that Eric won't believe me.

"Are you sure?"

"Positive. I need to get Fiducia out of there. She looked so sad and hurt."

"What about your sister?"

I lower my head. "She didn't survive the transformation."

He places his hand on my knee. "Sorry. It must be hard, like she died twice."

I swallow a wad of tears, picturing Fiducia. "They aren't savages like the news makes them out to be."

"I never thought they were."

There. That's why I told Eric.

But as I really look at him, there's no shock on his face. "You knew?"

"Yes."

I don't think I can handle any more surprises today. "How?"

"That's a story for another time. Is Fiducia okay?"

A part of me wants to prod Eric on how he knew about the Immundus, but I know there are more important things to worry about. "I don't know how I'm getting Fiducia out without my dad noticing."

"Have you told her parents?"

Her parents would probably be more shocked than I am and might tell people what Genesis did to her daughter, or worse, be eliminated before they get the chance. "I can't. I shouldn't have even told you, but I didn't know who else to turn to."

"Where would Fiducia go once you got her out?"

I throw my head back in frustration. "You're right. If I free her, everyone will know the truth."

"They *should* know the truth."

"You promised you wouldn't say anything."

"I won't. She might not want to come out, though. You said she was Immundus now. People would react differently to her. She might be afraid of people not accepting her. And you won't be able to hide her." He grabs my shoulders. "Talk to Fiducia first, see what she wants."

"If I talk to her, it will have to be now when the majority of scientists are out."

"Then go." He thrusts his arm forward.

"You're right." My heart jumps. I leap toward him, planting a kiss on his cheek. "Thank you."

"There's nothing to thank."

"Yes, there is. You're always there when I need you."

"Stop it. You're making me blush," he jokes, and for a period, the world is lit up by his smirk—the one I haven't seen in months. I smile back before I turn to go.

"Nia."

I turn back toward him. "Yeah?"

"Be careful."

TWELVE

KASHMIR AND KAFIRA

Back at Genesis, I try to recall the direction we went to see Fiducia. I step into the intersection of two long hallways. The walls are slightly beige and soothing music streams through the halls. I go straight. This isn't the same hall where I saw Fiducia. I must have taken a wrong turn. Several doors with handles occupy both sides of the hallway, none of them with windows to peek in. I pull at the first door I come upon, but it's locked. I jiggle the handle, unsure what I'll say if someone is behind the door. Granted, I'm on my father's project now and technically have the right to be here. Plus we all work late hours—that's nothing new.

I fearlessly proceed to open doors, armed with my response. The next two doors are locked, but the door after those opens. The room— large, austere, with empty off-white walls—carries a smell of mud and sulfur and blood. The only adornment is a small picture of a man with a gun against the back wall. An elevated bed spans the center of the room. Another scent wafts by, not acrid but not sweet either, simply different. Machines surround the bed, which has arm and leg straps. I try not to imagine what they do to the Immundus here. Nausea is my new companion at Genesis.

In the corner is a machine with several buttons of various sizes and colors. Fascinated by the machine, I walk toward it. One of the buttons is an ostrich, so I press it to see what happens. A loud jolting sound resonates in the room, then a portion of the wall breaks away, gently scraping the ground as it opens to another hall.

This hall is dimly lit, like dusk. A musky odor fills the corridor. From what I can make out, there are no doors, at least none I can see. The distant sound of dripping water echoes, a calm steady rhythm, opposite to my own beating heart. This is definitely not where my father took me earlier. It's all manual with no chip panel recognition. Why are these containment areas different? Was this one of the first containment areas that are no longer in use?

At the end of the hall, lights illuminate the stairwell. I run down the steep staircase that stretches around the corner into a shorter hall and another set of steps. I'm glad I haven't run into anyone yet. Even if my presence is completely justified to other personnel, I'll still have to deal with my father in the aftermath.

At the bottom is a radiant light from a hallway with rooms—these rooms have windows. I approach the window of the first room with caution and peer into the darkness. Glowing eyes stare back at me from the far side of the room. The door to the room is modern. I hesitate to place my hand on the reader, knowing they would be able to read that I was here via my chip. No, I can't let fear rule me. I'm on Project Restoration now, and I have a right to be here. That's as good of a lie as any, I suppose. I push my palm onto the reader. The door clicks, opening the moment my hand touches the panel.

The room lights up, revealing an Immundus, but it's not Fiducia.

I catch a glare off the translucent wall that splits the room in half.

"Who are you?" he asks, his forehead drawing his eyebrows toward the bridge of his nose.

I creep closer. Again he tilts his head, his eyes narrowing in on mine.

"I'm Nia . . . What about you?"

"Your people refer to me as Immundus," he says in a gravelly tone. I peer into his hazel eyes. Human eyes. Hungry eyes. Eyes that speak a silent story of suffering.

"Yes, but what is your name?"

Something like surprise lights his face, but it's far too subtle a facial expression to call it that. "To my people, I am Kashmir."

"Hi, Kashmir." I raise one hand, then shove both hands into my lab coat pockets. "How long have you been here?"

"I don't know, but if I had to estimate, I would say months."

"Do you know why we have you here?"

"I was told I am being researched to help save the lives of children." *Genesis lies.*

"Oh, well, I actually came looking for Fidu . . . I mean Dasha, and I got lost." His eyes penetrate mine like he's trying to figure out who I am. "Just so you know, I'm not one of the scientists that has you down here, but I would like to learn more about you."

"Your appearance states otherwise."

"I'm an apprentice. If you let me, I can tell you what the other scientists might not have told you about us, and hopefully you can share the same with me."

"You think I am going to help you learn the weaknesses of my people so you can capture more of us?" he asks.

"That's not what I said." I shake my head in frustration.

His eyes take hold of mine. "What is there to learn about me that you can't use against my people?"

"Tell me about your family." I lean forward and clasp my hands eager to hear his response. "Do you have any?"

"Why does it matter if I have family?" He turns toward a bookcase and glides his fingers along the spines of the books lining one of the middle shelves as though they were the strings of a guitar.

"How can it not?"

He stares at me silently.

"Okay . . . I'll go first. I have a mom who left when I was young, and grandparents and a sister who are dead. As for aunts and uncles, my mother is an only child and my father has a brother who lives in Genus Voluptas. I never met my uncle."

"I see," Kashmir replies in a condescending tone and takes a seat.

I stand and step toward the shield, placing my hands flat against the invisible wall. "What do you see?"

He says nothing. He just sits there looking at the bookcase, his hands resting on each knee.

"What do you see?" I raise my voice, but he still doesn't move or make a sound. I sigh and fall back into the chair.

"I see you have no family," he says, turning to me.

"I have family," I say, trying to convince him and myself. "I told you I have a father who works here."

"I listened to what you said. You did not say you have a father."

"Well . . . I do." I look down and fidget with my nails. "It's your turn to tell me about your family."

"Yes. I have a family," he says.

"That's it? I gave you more details than that." His eyes glance away, his face sullen, as though a flood of memories wash over him. I imagine that's what my painful memories must look like on the outside, throwing my feelings of safety and security to the wind.

"Why are you so calm? For someone who's been locked up for a few months, I would think you would be more hostile."

"For what purpose would I be otherwise?"

For the last several years I've been in combat training and watching news reports that cause us to believe Immundus are a danger. Yet one stands before me—one that I do not have any personal ties to—devoid of anger for what we've done, engulfed in concern for his family and his people. Instead, we are the danger. We are the ones caging them like animals. Not much has changed over a millennia. Our human nature compels us to repeat the same mistakes, regardless of how much we try to avoid it. How different are we now if we still devalue the lives of sentient beings by treating them as lesser beings? What gives us the right to say our lives are more valuable than the Immundus? My heart falls into a chasm of grief for Kashmir and his kind.

My stomach growls, reminding me that I skipped dinner. I made the choice not to eat so I could search these halls for Fiducia. In the time

I've been down here with Kashmir, no one has brought him food and there're no empty dishes in his cell.

"Have you eaten?" I ask.

"You have the look of someone quite concerned for my well-being. Tell me. Why do you care?"

"I care because you should be treated well."

"And what is treated well in your mind?" Kashmir says, walking toward the sheer wall that divides us.

"Being fed, letting you take showers and use a restroom . . ."

"Would you like to know what being treated well means to me?"

"Yes." The word shoots out my mouth in mezzo soprano.

"It means respecting others, regardless of whether they deserve the respect, because you value them for who they are, a being," he says.

"Even a murderer?"

"Yes, even those who come into this room every day."

"What? We don't kill." I cross my arms, immediately defensive, but I'm uncertain even as I say it. My dad used tranquilizers during hunting at least, but what else do I really know? They killed Derek, why wouldn't they kill an Immundus?

Kashmir remains peacefully apathetic, sitting there in our Sapiens clothing. In response, he slowly lifts up his shirt, revealing a raw patch of flesh, as though someone rubbed a grater across it. He raises his shirt even further—more scars, welts, and raw tissue blanket his skin, some appearing fresh from that day. Evidence against my protest.

"Does it hurt? I mean, do you still feel tenderness or pain now?"

"Perhaps the better question is *what hurt more?*" he states, lowering his shirt.

"Why?" I ask. The light flickers in the hall, drawing my attention. A deep mildew smell wafts in.

"Physical pain can be unbearable at the moment it is felt and for weeks, months, even years later, but the body is resilient and will work to heal itself. The mind, however, can never truly be healed. An experience cannot be forgotten. We simply learn to live with it." He pauses and glances around the room. "I was brought here and put in this room. Tortured. But it was not as painful as knowing that, to Sapiens, I was nothing more than an object. A tool to accomplish what Sapiens want."

I fight back tears wrestling to escape my eyes, but I know he's right. I fractured my leg as a child. My mom was around, so she sent me to see a naturologist. Now I run, jump, and dance and never feel anything that reminds me of my fracture. But the departure of my mom from my life creeps into the forefront of my mind, one continuous cycle, without regard for necessity or purpose.

"I'm sorry," I say.

"Did you do this to me?"

"No." Although the word spills from my lips, I somehow feel responsible.

"Then why are you apologizing to me?"

"I'm sorry for my kind. I'm sorry we're not creative, intelligent, or compassionate enough to think of non-barbaric ways to do things. I'm sorry that your value is distorted by our egotistical desires. I'm sorry we still haven't learned from past mistakes."

"Be sorry not for your kind but for your own actions and what you do with the knowledge that you have acquired."

With all that my species has done to him, he should be angry. I would be gnarling at every person who approached me if it were the other way around. But he is calm; his hollow eyes invite me into his despair. Immundus are obviously the next evolution of man. They are better than we are.

A sudden shiver radiates up my spine, fingers of a cold breeze sweep up across my back. What if he isn't here to help us "cure" the Immundus condition, but to help us know how to kill his species entirely? Darwinism's survival of the fittest in full swing: Sapiens being the ones attempting to out-survive the Immundus, even those we love who become them. We are a self-hating species.

I contemplate him. I know I need to go back home now. "I'll be back tomorrow."

"Did you learn everything you know from one teacher?"

"No."

"Perhaps, if you want to learn of my people, your time would be best suited to meeting others down here. After all, one cannot comprehend a subject by reading one book. You have much to learn, apprentice." I love the way he speaks, his reticent yet powerful tone, reminds me of a martial arts master of times past.

"I will look for others tomorrow." I nod and shut the door.

· · ● ● ● · ·

A part of me loves the work in my father's lab. As a scientist, it's the greatest challenge of all—keeping one species alive at the sake of the other. Perhaps that's what makes it easier for him and the rest of them. They are fascinated. It's a fascination that has moved the dial on their moral compass, unbeknownst to them, amidst their awe and wonder. Now I am waiting. Waiting. Waiting. Waiting for the day to be over so I can go see another Immundus, maybe even find Fiducia's new location. My father must have moved her.

I pour a chemical into the tube, mix it, then set the tube into its tray. The lights in the room begin to dim, so I wave my hands around to relight it. Empty seats deck the lab. Silence jams into every nook of space; a silence I didn't know could exist in this space. My father is held behind the doors of his office by his own family's guilt. I don't even know if the other teams are gone for the day.

My dad must know what I did last night and what I'll do again tonight. But I'm his legacy, so he's keeping me safe from whoever killed Derek. *Unless he killed Derek to keep his own secret.*

I skulk down the dingy staircase toward the corridor where the Immundus are held. The regular elevator that leads to the cafeteria, joey, and ostrich levels doesn't stop on this floor. I approach the cells. A croaky voice catches my ears, and I stretch my head toward the edge of the wall, listening. I can't make out what the person is saying, it sounds deep and muffled. Lead footsteps vibrate against the walls, each plodded step diminishing the farther away the person moves. The elevator dings, the person steps in.

I wait a moment. While I have clearance for being here, I know my father would be furious that I'm spending time to try to get to know the Immundus. If he asks, I could tell him that I'm studying them in order to identify if any personality changes might help me figure out how to stop the gene from activating or removing it altogether. I figure I can make *something* up. But I'd rather avoid being seen by others down here if I can help it. The fewer times I have to explain myself, the better.

Finally, I move forward. A few more steps and I peer into Kashmir's window. He's alone, pacing back and forth, like before. I enter the room and Kashmir's eyes pounce mine.

"Come to read the same book?" he asks.

"No, but I did want to say hi."

He stares at me and says nothing. I shrug and sweep out of his door and back into the hall. I walk past the other rooms, glancing in their windows. Each room has one Immundus, pacing back and forth, seated or lying down. I am transported into their circumstance, shackled by an abysmal sense of despair.

Most Immundus are adults, females and males, except three, who appear to be children. Part of me wants to visit with the children. I pause for a moment, watching one of them play with a puzzle. I know that if I'm going to learn anything that will help them, it'll be from an elder Immundus. I skulked back through the musky-smelling hall, examining each Immundus, trying to figure out who the eldest is. They look analogous in age. I notice one who looks tired, so I enter that room. She doesn't move. Her droopy eyes gaze upon the floor. I watch tears trickle down her face, landing on her shirt. She clears her throat the way I do, attempting to hold back a rush of tears. My heart sinks into a chasm. Should I say something?

"Hello." The word floats out, like the soft clouds that form from the weather machine.

She shifts toward me—her eyes despondent.

"I'm Nia." She doesn't respond. Her empty gaze crushes my spirit. I am angry all over again—why are we doing this to them? I don't want to feel this way. I turn away for a moment to catch myself from being swallowed by her despair. I want to step out, but then she speaks.

"What do you want of me?" Her voice drifts like a sparrow's song.

"I don't know . . ." I mutter. *What do I want from them? What do I feel for them?*

"Do you know who I am?" she asks.

"You're an Immundus."

"That is not what I asked, yet it is apparent that is all you see," she says, saddened by my response.

"I'm sorry." I draw nearer to the shield. "Please tell me who you are."

"It is not for me to tell you who I am, but for you to know it for yourself." She speaks like Kashmir.

"I don't understand," I admit. "How do I know it for myself?"

"You must be the one to figure it out if you are ever going to know who I am." Her tone as smooth as almond milk.

She wraps her arms behind her and begins to pace. "Would you speak to me if I had no voice? Would you make any effort to communicate with me or would you walk away and view me as a being of less value than you?" Her questions dig their way into the canals of my mind, searching, seeking out some answer that will quell her questions and restore some semblance of intellect on my part. But I have no answers, only questions: *What would I do? Would I still talk to her? Would I make any effort to communicate with her?*

"I don't know," falls from my lips again. I'm getting nowhere. "What's your name?" I blurt out.

"Kafira," she says.

She was waiting for me to ask. I'm beginning to realize the significance of not even thinking to ask—and what that means.

"Who am I?" she asks again.

This time I feel a bit more confident that I know the answer.

"You're Kafira, an Immundus woman," I say with pomp.

"Still you use your eyes which do not provide true sight," she says. "Tell me what blinds you."

"I don't understand the question," I say. I almost nibble on my thumbnail but stop myself mid crunch. "I came to learn from you . . . to learn about you."

"For what purpose do you seek this knowledge?" she inquires, her eyes arrested with interest.

"To understand if you want the cure," I say.

She waits, as if she expects me to say more. When I don't, she says, "Then you are not ready for the knowledge that you seek."

What? That doesn't make sense. "Why? Isn't that enough? To want to know if you even want the cure that places you in this cage?"

"We are more than your cure. Go now and do not return until you are ready to learn."

"How do I know I'm ready?" I ask with rutted brow.

"You are the sole person who can answer that," she says, rising.

I exit and call Eric. I need his insight again. He told me to talk to Fiducia to see what she wants, but I can't find her, so here I am, talking with Kafira—and it's not enough.

THIRTEEN

CONFESSIONS

The park is dark, lit only by the stars that surround the edge. Like last time, Eric is swaying on a swing.

The moment I see him, I'm seized by the urge to get close to him like we were, for a brief moment, by his car, but that's not fair to him. I don't understand why I feel the need to take over his space, to have him touch me. Maybe I'm just under too much stress. Maybe I'm looking for comfort in the one place I know I won't be denied it. But I stay back, away from him, and jump right into our conversation.

"I wasn't able to find Fiducia, but I was able to visit with two Immundus—Kashmir and Kafira." I glance around to make sure no one can overhear us; it's not exactly the kind of talk you can have in the open. "I've tried to get to know them, but I can't make it past their questioning. It's like I have to pass a test before they'll tell me anything."

"What did they ask you?"

"Kafira wants me to tell her who she is and why I want to learn about the Immundus."

"And? What did you say?"

"I told her she's a female Immundus, and I want to learn if the Immundus actually want a cure. What's wrong with that answer?"

He looks down for a moment, swinging back and forth, searching for a response. I feel comfort in knowing he's interested in helping me figure them out and not taking it lightly by giving a quick answer—he's thinking it through. Then he says something unexpected.

"Who are you?"

"Who am I?"

"Yeah . . . who are you?" he persists.

"I'm Nia. You know that."

"Is that all?"

"Yes." I draw out the word, unsure of my answer.

"So your name is who you are?"

"No. I'm the daughter of John and Rosemary."

"So your parents define who you are?"

"No. What are you getting at?" I say, flustered, feeling like I'm back in the room with Kafira.

"Do you think that it's hard for you to know who she is because you don't even know yourself?"

My mind repeats the question *Who am I?* I think about it for a moment.

"Who are you, Eric?"

"I would hope you know, but I'm a compassionate person who loves life, not only my own, but all life. I love my family, and I'm in love with a girl who's emotionally unavailable," he says, his passionate stare piercing my heart. "And I have hope that one day I'll meet my mother who left me and my father after I was born. I'm more than a Homo sapiens. The label doesn't define me. I am infinite. I am a creature of the world, trying to find my way like every other creature that's ever had the pleasure to exist."

I feel small, intimidated by his passion but inspired to be better than my self-deprecating thoughts would have me be. I think over his answer. It reflects each piece of him—some I knew, some I didn't know. I skip over his love for me because I feel like I can't breathe when I focus on it. Then I land on what's bothering me. I don't understand why he wants to meet his mother . . . I can't forgive mine for leaving me.

"Aren't you in pain from your mother abandoning you?" My pain is so great that I don't admit I want to see my mother again. I know I do, but it's easier to hold on to my anger instead. I don't understand how Eric is at peace with his own abandonment.

"I was, but I forgave her. I know she left for a reason. I make choices every day that I act on. Each choice deliberate, like when I told you I loved you. And I have to face the consequences of each of those choices." He gulps. "My mom's dealing with the consequence of leaving me and my dad. But I can't deny that her departure brought my stepmom, Jennifer, and my brothers and sisters into my life. How can I hate her for that?"

His words caress my heart. Mrs. Marcello, who was one of my Futures instructors, has been his mom since I have known him. I don't have the luxury of a new mom, not with a father consumed in his work. Who would want to put up with that?

"So Kafira wants me to see her as more than just an Immundus? More than just a woman and a name?" I ask.

"I think so," he says.

"But what about the reason that I was there? Why didn't she accept that I was there to just know whether or not they wanted the cure?"

"She could have been more concerned with what you wanted to do with the knowledge . . . to help her and her people . . . or to deceive and harm them. She might have thought you were sent to test them. Sent to see who was rebellious."

"Honestly—I just want to get to know her as a person."

"That's a start. Did you tell her?"

"No." The word, a tight-wound ball of regret, bounces out of my mouth.

"Listen," he says, brushing my hairs from my face, a thing he does even though my hair doesn't bother me. "I know that you're more than just a scientist, more than just a person who will fall in line and look at test tubes, never wondering what pain came along with their contents." He stops his swing and mine, taking my hands into his. "I know that you care about life. That if the way to help our species survive is by hurting an Immundus, you won't."

"How do you know that? What if I'm not who you think I am?" He doesn't know I went hunting for Immundus with my dad—I couldn't bear to tell him that I drove the car and did nothing to stop my father—that I even helped load the bodies into the car.

"I know you. As much as you might try to hide it, I can see the pain in your eyes, in your gestures, in your posture during certain conversations . . . like now," he says with such surety, his tender voice lulling my frustration. "And I have something else to tell you, too."

I lean into the swing's chain, curious as to what he needs to tell me. What greater secret can there be than his love for me? A love I still don't know what to do with. I snap to attention when he continues.

"I trust you with my life, Nia."

I wasn't expecting that. "That's kind of dire, don't you think?"

"I'm serious." His voice takes on a stern tone.

"Okay," I say apologetically.

"I . . . I think the best way to tell you is to show you." Eric pulls up his navy shirt, revealing his torso, and before I can even attempt to turn away—if I even could—I see it: iridescent skin sprinkled with multiple colors. Immundus skin.

I stare at his skin, mesmerized. I can't believe it. My fingers inch forward of their own volition, sliding across the scales. Chills percolate on my arms. "How is this possible?"

Then an explanation occurs to me. "Eric, what stopped you from transforming completely?"

"I didn't change at all," he says, grasping my shoulders, his eyes meeting mine. "I've had this since I was born."

"Since you were born?" My mind races—a cacophony of competing thoughts bombard me. How could his condition have slipped through the birther's radar?

"Since I was born. I have other patches just like this on other areas of my body. That's why whenever we changed for the games I used the dressing room. And why we had to stay away from Genesis."

"We?"

"My father is a Genesis legacy. During his apprenticeship he met and fell in love with an Immundus girl. I'm the result of their relationship. I'm alive because of my grandfather—he spared us for the sake of his son. He kept it quiet and helped my mother to escape, to return to her people, and my dad was allowed to keep me, but needed to immediately find a new employer. It was too risky for our secret to be so close to Genesis."

"But you just told me your mom abandoned you."

"In a way, she did. She had to. Not in the same way that your mom abandoned you, but the bottom line is both of our mothers are alive and not with us."

"Oh, Eric, this—living here—couldn't have been easy," I say.

"It wasn't, but now that you know, if you think I'm impure, then you can turn me in to your father. But if you think I'm more than my skin, I'll stay by your side and help you to figure all this out. Either way, my life is in your hands now." His words are thick with melancholy and a tint of shame.

I feel pain at Eric's words. My heart fractures at the thought that he would ever think I would consider him less for his skin, his beautiful tapestry of skin, or for who his mother is. I know some would, like my father, but not me—never me.

"You know you are more than your flesh," I say, lifting his chin, our eyes capturing each other's. I recall something my mother said when I was a little girl. "There will be a time we will live beyond the confines of our bone and muscle cages. When it will no longer be requisite to use this life support system . . ." I touch my heart with his hand. ". . . and we can shed these skins—our temporary costumes."

He smiles, revealing his dimple. "That's one of the reasons I'm in love with you and always have been."

Eric's right hand reaches out for mine, stroking my fingertips, soft, subtle, and sliding into position, intertwining his fingers with my own, his thumb caressing my hand. I examine our hands, connected, and a surge of warmth rushes through my body, my heart flutters, and my stomach tingles. I gaze at our hands for a short time and think about the trust he has in me, the trust needed to tell me his profound secret. And I think again on how he bared himself, even if he was afraid I'd betray him. As if I could ever love Eric less.

In that split second I discover: I love Eric.

I'm *in love* with Eric.

Tears well up and for the first time, the shackles of fear fall from me. The tears are an amalgamation of relief, love, and joy. Finally, I'm not alone. I'm no longer alone.

"Nia?" Eric asks, wiping at my tears.

"Eric." I heave in a breath, then say what I couldn't contain if I tried. "I'm in love with you, too."

His smile is so bright it can light our genus. "And this is why you're crying?"

"Yes," I say, attempting to stop my embarrassing flood. He dries my moist face, the tenderness of his fingers strum my heart. "But they're happy tears. I feel like I don't have to be afraid anymore—afraid of loving, afraid of my fears, afraid of loss, afraid of being discovered for the lost creature I feel I am. Because I'm not alone in my journey," I say, allowing the full force of my thoughts and emotions to run free. I hold his cheeks within my palms and dive into his eyes. "I love you. I love you beyond flesh, beyond bone, beyond this costume you wear. I love the person I experience when that's all stripped away. I love you, Eric—and I'm sorry it took me so long to acknowledge it."

I inch forward, pausing just short of our lips touching and take in his breath. The moment expands and stretches until our lips meet. It's a dance, a sweet ballet, and I'm aware of every feeling that comes with it. A flurry of stimulation cascades down my body, every cell celebrating and screaming *I love you*. He runs his hand through my hair, sparking more fantastical sensations. I never want to disconnect my lips from his, as though being lost is no longer a bad idea, as long as I'm lost with him. He draws back and gives me an endearing kiss on the tip of my nose. Our eyes meet again. And I can't imagine how I ever thought I didn't always love Eric.

"I love you, Nia! I love you beyond flesh," he says, pulling my swing close to him, wrapping me in the warmth of his comforting embrace. I breathe him in and indulge in the starry sky. We sit in silence and I think about how glad I am that my first kiss was with him—with someone I love.

"That's what you need to tell the Immundus, you know," Eric says in the quiet of night.

"What?"

"Nia, you have this ability to experience people with intuitiveness, beyond their fleshy cages, but you hide it. Don't hide that gift—that's what the Immundus want to hear."

"You're right! Eric, you're right!" I stand in a rush, but his hand reaches out and grabs onto mine. It tingles where our skin touches.

"Tomorrow." He tugs me closer. "For tonight, let's stay here," he says.

"In the park?"

"Yes." The word nearly explodes from his chest.

I smile. I don't have anywhere else to be—not now. And there isn't anywhere else I want to be.

"Okay."

His face beams brighter than the moonlight. "I'll run to my house and get us some blankets and pillows," he says.

I nod. His right hand lifts my chin. He kisses me—his lips soft as they press into mine—then runs off toward his house.

I sit alone, swinging, my mind lingering on the sweetness of his lips. I don't want to let go of the feeling. If only I could hold onto that feeling forever—a tornado of pure joy swirling inside me. I'm sure if anyone is watching me right now, they'd think I'm weird, sitting alone in the park on a swing with a super-sized smile imprinted on my face. But that's okay. I'm happy.

Eric returns with two sleeping bags and pillows. He opens both bags, using one as the bed and the other as our blanket.

"Eric? Just sleeping, right?"

He turns beet-red, but looks me in the eye anyway. "Yup. Just that."

"Okay, then," I say with a smile that crinkles my eyes. We settle in, and I nestle my head on his steely chest. He wraps his arms around me and lets out a long, contented sigh. I hide my smile against his shirt.

I try to relish this moment, so rare in my long, lonely span of living. Joy like this is often fleeting and met with the opposition of things gone wrong. I suppose that's life. But I'd like to feel like I have some sense of control. In Eric's arms, I convince myself that I do.

I will keep this, I promise myself. *I will protect this from breaking.*

In his arms I find a peace I have never known—as though the world has faded away and he and I are alone in a soft billowy blanket among the stars and moon, and the sound of the wind through the trees serenades us into a blissful sleep.

FOURTEEN

FIDUCIA

I awake to the music of the trees. I crack open my eyes, enamored with the light pink blossoms of a nearby tree, the shapely form of its branches dancing in the wind, the leaves caressing each other with each sway—the tree, a creator and conductor of its own music. The sun hasn't breached the wall yet, creating vibrant shades of red across the sky, heralding the birth of day. Last night, Eric had gotten sleeping bags so we could sleep under the stars, entwined in each other's arms. I glance at my forearm to determine the time, realizing I forgot to set an alarm for work. It's five thirty, so I still have time to get ready. I turn over to tell Eric but he's already awake and ogling me, his lips curled up a pinch. I pull the cover up and over the bottom portion of my face, embarrassed by my morning appearance, and to save him from my rancid breath.

"I have to get ready for work," I mumble, my words muffled by the cover.

"I know. So do I," he says, allowing his breath free reign, though I don't smell anything.

I feel his watchful gaze on me as I sit up and brush my hands through my tousled hair.

"Have breakfast with me and my family?" he asks.

"Are you sure?" I ask in a bit of shock, my words now muffled by my hand cupped over my mouth.

"Absolutely." He chuckles. "Meet me at my house at six forty-five."

I think for a moment. *Will I be able to make it to his house on time?* "I think I can do that." My words no longer muffled. I sprout up.

"Okay." He nods in acknowledgement. "I'll see you soon."

I scamper home, almost skipping—well, my version of skipping, anyway.

· · • ● • · ·

At home I get ready the fastest I think I ever have. It's quickly approaching the time I'm scheduled to meet Eric at his family's house. I hear a knock at my bedroom door. Of all the days my father chooses to approach my door, he does so on a day I don't have the time—or the inclination—to chat. I shut off the hologram door.

"I know you just got home. Where were you last night?"

A warm feeling encapsulates my body momentarily. I have so many confusing feelings about my father. I wonder if he's trapped by his own work—his own promises to his parents. I wonder if he's truly as cruel as he is when he is hunting. I don't know him, and that's the problem. But I don't think I've ever had so much of his focus on me before—or rather on my personal life. Is it possible that my dad actually cares?

"Eric and I camped out last night in the park."

"Eric?" He rubs his chin.

For a moment I see him as a mere father concerned about his child being out all night with a boy, but then I remember his eyes when we were hunting Immundus. Eric is part Immundus and sure to be a prize to my father. He must never learn about Eric. "My best friend, all through school," I finally reply.

"Yes, right."

I glance at the time on my forearm. I have five minutes to make it to Eric's house. "I have to go, I'm having breakfast at his house," I say, grabbing a lipstick and swiping the rosy pink shade across my lips. "I'll see you at work." I make it halfway down the stairs before he shouts that we can go to work together tomorrow—that we have things to discuss. I pause, as my stomach shoots up to my throat.

"Of course, John!" I reply.

· · • ● • · ·

I make it to Eric's house two minutes late. He's leaning against the doorway, his eyes capturing mine. His smile reels me in. My heart skips. "You made it."

He hugs my hands with his, presses his forehead to mine, his eyes engaging mine in a dance, easing any worries I might have in having breakfast with his family.

His home is the epitome of family. Pictures of his family adorn the cream-colored walls; their crinkled paper texture contrasting with the seashell white crown molding. I'm bombarded by a wave of warmth and tantalizing smells coming from the kitchen, causing my stomach to growl. His family is seated at the table. He has two sisters, Audrey and Alyson, and one brother, Todd—all average looking. Another brother Craig has been living in Genus Voluptas for the last two years. My body shudders at the thought that Eric could have been living in Genus Voluptas had he not responded contrary to his nature on the career tests.

"Welcome, Nia!" says Mrs. Marcello. "We have a seat saved for you." She gestures to a worn wooden chair with floral etchings and a deep blue cushion. It must have been Craig's seat. She nods to Eric who pulls out the chair for me.

"Thank you!" I shrug a shoulder. I hope the others don't recognize my embarrassment, but the rush of blood I feel engorging my face tells me otherwise. I don't know why I'm embarrassed; Eric has always been chivalrous—doing things like giving up his seat for me. I suppose it's because he's doing this in front of his family, all seated and ready to eat.

The tile table is set with food across the crimson center table runner: three bowls of biscuits, potatoes, and salad. A pitcher of orange juice tops off the meal. Everyone else has already served themselves and are waiting on me. Just seeing his family makes me sad about my own. I don't remember the last time my father and I sat down at a table at home to eat.

"Go ahead and serve what you want," says Mrs. Marcello. I place a helping of potatoes on my plate and take a biscuit but skip the salad. I don't see salad as breakfast food. I look around to see who'll eat first since I don't want to be the first one to eat the delights.

"Who would like to say prayer today?" Mr. Marcello asks. My eyes pop at the thought someone might nominate me. My mom used to pray. She would tuck me into bed and pray with me, then sing me a lullaby until I drifted off to sleep. I continued praying before I went to sleep for around a year after she left, hoping I would get some answer, but nothing came. Prayer didn't help either of us, so I haven't felt the need to pray since.

"I'll pray," says Eric, glancing at me from his peripheral vision before shutting his eyes and grasping my hand. I close my eyes and listen to his words to a God that I am not sure exists. He ends, looks up, and kisses me with his eyes. "Let's eat."

I get one bite in and Mr. Marcello asks, "So how are things at Genesis?" I nearly choke but quickly chase my food down with a drink to respond. Mrs. Marcello scolds him for not giving me a chance to eat. Mr. Marcello knows exactly how anyone's time at Genesis goes, but perhaps since I'm a first-year apprentice, he assumes I don't. Either way, I'm guessing neither of us can be honest about our time at Genesis with the rest of his family at the table.

"I . . . well, there's certainly a lot to still learn as an apprentice."

"Yes, there is." His response is abrupt and there's a glare in his eyes, making me feel that he's somewhat put off by me. The thought saddens me.

"Do you know my father, Mr. Marcello?" I ask, hoping he'll say yes and put me at ease that he's redirecting old feelings for my father toward me.

"Yes, I do," he says.

"Did you ever work with him on a project when you worked at Genesis?" He looks up, surprised at my question. I'm surprised at it myself. This isn't the place to air these grievances.

"I—"

"Dad, I told her. She knows about me being part Immundus. And she's experienced some stuff on her own. She's on our side," Eric chimes in.

"Yes . . . I'm on your side," I echo Eric's statement, unsure what my words mean.

"Do you know what it means to *be* on our side?" I guess Mr. Marcello picked up on my uncertainty.

"Steve, let's eat in peace. I'm sure Nia didn't come over to be interrogated over breakfast. There will be time enough to talk," Mrs. Marcello orders.

"I am just . . ." Mr. Marcello begins to speak, but Mrs. Marcello swings in a stare that bars his mouth from shedding another word.

Eric leans in, whispering in my ear, "It's okay, trust me."

We continue eating in silence, but the question of what "sides" means burns a hole in my mouth. As much as I want Mrs. Marcello to have her peaceful morning breakfast, I want to know what Eric and Mr. Marcello referred to when they talked about sides. It sounded like it was more than me keeping Eric's secret. But how do I ask without alienating myself, making myself look like an intruder?

"I don't know what you're referring to by sides. But I can tell you what I know. I know that Genesis is capturing and running tests on the Immundus. And I know the Immundus are being told they're helping us to find a cure for allagine—a disorder that doesn't exist," I say, half out of breath. When I mention the Immundus, none of them even flinch an eye. It makes sense, given their family history. Given Eric's birth mother. But it's still surprising, outside of my father's project, to me.

"How did you find out about the Immundus?" Mr. Marcello asks.

"I'm working in my father's lab."

Mr. Marcello leans forward, his arms resting on the table, parallel to the runner. "You're a first-year apprentice. How did you manage to get yourself on your dad's confidential project?"

"There was an elevator malfunction. On the ostrich floor. An Immundus briefly escaped and ran by before the doors closed. I just saw a flash—I didn't even know what I was seeing until my friend was dead and I was on my dad's project."

"Your father did what he could to save you. The Domus Council runs Genesis—and they don't care for anyone to know their secrets." He glances at Eric, then back to me. "They put you on your father's project so he can keep an eye on you. It must have been your father's guarantee to them."

"I'd figured as much." My stomach shifts into an uneasiness. I'm no longer hungry. I think Eric notices the glowering look on my face because he places his hand on mine, as gentle as a soft snowfall. Mrs. Marcello brings the conversation around to a more pleasant one regarding a day trip with the other family members to the animal museum since it's summer break. Eric's other siblings and Mrs. Marcello, who still teaches Futures, have one month off. Mr. Marcello and Eric will be at work, so they won't go.

"It's getting close to eight o'clock. You should all be heading to work about now," Mrs. Marcello says in her motherly tone.

"Thank you for breakfast," I say.

Mr. Marcello, Eric, and I rise from the table and head out the front door. I feel awkward about kissing Eric since his mom is at the door seeing us all off. Instead I give him a hug and get into my car.

· · • ● • · ·

When I get to the office, it feels more crucial than ever to find Fiducia today. I check in at my station and then head to the hidden floor, where she must be—somewhere. I pass Kashmir's, then Kafira's door. I let my instincts guide me this time, like I did in the Spero games, and they send me through various turns until I'm farther into the maze of this floor. I've walked all these halls; I've tried so many doors. But today, something tells me I'll finally find her. I stop at a door on my right that seems to be drawing me in. I reach for the knob and turn it, holding my breath and hoping this is the room where I will find Fiducia.

I push out a sigh of relief. I found her!

She's sitting on a cot, holding another book. Her head turns sharply when I enter. I know, without a doubt, that my father will not let me linger here. He might let me loiter in other cells, but he knows this is too powerful, too important to me. I have minutes before I need to head back to the lab, so we cannot have the reunion I want. Instead, I know I need to use this time to find the answer I've been seeking.

Our eyes meet. "Fiducia."

Her eyes shut briefly and then reopen. "I haven't heard that name in a long time."

"I'm sorry."

"Why are you sorry? I don't mind hearing it."

"No, I'm sorry because you're here," I nod to her arm, which looks as if it's been freshly raked, "and because they hurt you."

She watches me silently. "They?"

"Yes, *they*. And they will come and pull me from here any minute now, so I need to ask you a question, Fiducia. And I know you have no reason to trust me, but right now, I need you to."

"What is your question?"

"If there was a cure, if there was a way to reverse your transformation, to make you Sapiens instead of Immundus, would you want it?"

She hesitates a moment. "Would I get to see my parents again?"

"It makes no difference. There's no guarantee you get to see your parents either way."

Her eyes shut again and she sighs. I'm sorry to cause her more pain, but if I'm ever going to help her get what she wants, I need an answer—one not affected by the idea of reuniting with her parents.

"I need to know for you and you alone. Would you want it?"

There's no hesitation this time. "No. I do not need it. I do not want it. Because I am not sick, I simply *am*."

There's a moment of silence when I hear this, when I hear the words that chew up my world and spit it out into a new configuration. The words that confirm that the Immundus don't want or need this cure, but that we do—that we are causing suffering for the sake of our species dominance and continued existence. I don't even know how Fiducia knows this truth—they no doubt lied to her as they do to the rest of the genus—but somehow she's seen through it.

"Then what do you need, Fiducia? What do you want?"

At the question, she scans me a moment before standing up and coming to the translucent shield that separates us. She places one palm on it, flat against the shield.

"Freedom."

FIFTEEN

ATTEMPT

I can't get Fiducia's final word out of my head all morning. Freedom. How can I possibly give her that? I'm just a girl. An apprentice.

I left immediately after her answer, unsure what to say, and worked at my station the rest of the day. I tried not to think about the scales I was handling, fighting down my nausea—each piece reminding me of Fiducia. By the end of the day, I knew that I couldn't let her spend one more night in her cell. I have to get her out and I have an idea how to do so.

Instead of going home after work, I ask Jules to order the unique adhesive used to hold the earwrap during Spero and the special liquid that removes it, from the commissary. Thankfully they're open twenty-four hours a day.

There's no line at the commissary, so the cart comes out as soon as we pull up. Jules's trunk arms reach out, grab the items from the cart, and pull them in, placing them into my hands. On the way back to Genesis, I turn on my media chip to watch movie clips of people broken out of prison. We don't have Sapiens prisons anymore, but the cells in Genesis look like a prison to me.

My favorite movie clip is from *The Count of Monte Cristo*, when the main character, Edmond Dantes, escapes from prison in a body bag intended for someone else. The guards toss the body bag into the sea, where Edmond wriggles free and swims to his freedom. Unfortunately, my dad said that they burn the dead Immundus bodies, so I can't put Fiducia into a body bag for this escape.

"We have arrived at Genesis," Jules announces.

I turn off the media chip. "Thanks, Jules. Park around the corner. I need to wait a bit longer before I go in." I turn the media chip back on and return to watching the video clips.

At midnight, I have Jules take me to the garage entrance. Jules flashes her lights like usual, but this time nothing happens.

I wonder whether the garage doors lock after a certain time, and if so, how am I going to get in? *What would I do in Spero?* I have to work through this. I know that Jules has the sensor that allows her flash to open the doors so she has special access like I do. My dad has been at work later than midnight, so maybe he's still in his office, which means Jaden is in the garage. But if we contact Jaden, she might tell my dad. I shake my head. I have to get in. The risk is worth it.

"Jules, ask Jaden if she's in the Genesis garage." Pools of sweat form on my palms.

"Okay. Please hold while I attempt to connect."

My heart races. I look around nervously. Fortunately, there's nobody around. I wait. Jules says nothing. Am I doing the right thing? Should I even be here? What if they find out it was me who took Fiducia? Jules doesn't give me time to talk myself out of this rescue.

"Jaden informed me that after midnight, a series of flashes must occur in the proper cadence to open the door. Would you like me to show you?"

"Yes." I exhale in one giant breath of relief.

The garage door opens and after I speak the code, Jules and I ride to my dad's lab's level where the elevator at the front entrance doesn't go, probably because that holds Immundus. After Jules parks, I stick the glue and glue remover in my pocket and head straight for the cages. I'm counting on security thinking I'm coming here to work. The halls are darker than usual because there is no light emanating from the cells—everyone's asleep. I pull out a maglite that I had grabbed from my father's desk earlier that day. I jog through the route I took last time to Fiducia's cage. Once I remove the barrier, I know I won't have much time, so I pause just outside her door and chug down some courage before placing my hand on the knob.

The door is locked.

I flash the maglite through the window and see Fiducia sleeping. I knock gently on the window, then harder, to get her attention. She shifts in bed and looks up. Now that she knows I'm here, I work on jimmying the lock, but it's not as easy as I thought. I realize I might have to break the window. There's no metal in these halls so I run back up to the entry room to this hidden level, where I remember seeing a tray hooked to a large pole. I snatch the pole and blow down the steps and back to Fiducia.

I place the maglite in my mouth, aiming it at the window, and grip the pole in my hands, raising it high like a bat. I feel my heartbeat in my ears and count down. *One . . . Two . . .* I swing. But the pole's caught mid air by a hand. I drop the maglite.

"What do you think you're doing?" Anger streams from every booming syllable. I can't see the face, but I know it's my father. My heart feels like it's trying to escape my chest, this hall, and Genesis.

"I'm giving Fiducia what she wants. Freedom." I can hear the fear trickling between the anger and disgust of my words.

"No, you're not, Nia. You're giving *my* bosses a reason to remove you from this project. And I know we both don't want that." The memory of Derek flashes in my mind and I realize what he means by that. It's my life or hers. "You are going to go home right now, and I expect to see you in the lab at the usual time tomorrow."

What courage I had earlier shrinks to nonexistence. What was I thinking? I had no real plan, except for putting glue on the door handles as we escaped. I didn't know about the garage door or that her door would be locked late at night. "How did you know I was down here?"

"Jaden told me. I knew the only reason you'd come here this late is to see Fiducia, but I didn't think you would try to set her free. You have to think, Nia, about the consequences of your actions."

Jaden, ugh. I say nothing. He's trying to protect me. So I pick up my maglite from the floor and trudge back to Jules, but not before stealing one last look of Fiducia.

· · • ● • · ·

As soon as I get into work, my father says nothing about last night but asks me to join him on another hunt, and it was almost a relief not to be looking at some Immundus skin that might be Fiducia's, until I remember the point of the trip.

Driving out of the genus has been the only redeeming factor of these hunting trips. I hate them, but I do my best to hide my feelings so it's not evident on my face. I try to focus on seeing the different trees and flowers, at least until I can figure out how to avoid the trips altogether. And I'm glad my dad has let me drive while *he* does the shooting, and Ryan, one of the other lab workers, has been joining us to lift the bodies in and out of the car, both of which have kept my guilt at bay. I keep thinking about Kashmir and Kafira. Is this how they were taken?

We're out farther than usual, having not found an Immundus. Giggles ride the air—not ours—yet nothing is in sight.

"Stop the vehicle," my dad says. "Zoom in on the surrounding area."

I adjust the controls on my forearm, then scan the area. I spot the backs of three children and an adult Immundus. They are moving.

"Today is your turn, Nia." He places a loaded tranquilizer in my hand. My heart bursts into an accelerated rhythm, and I break out in a sweat.

"What?"

"I said it's your turn. I'll go for the adult. Ryan will go for the two Immundus in the middle and you'll aim for the one on the far right. We have to time this right because once one is shot the others will scatter. None of them can make it back to where they came from."

I gulp down the bile that's rising in my throat. This is probably payback for last night. I can't do this. Maybe I can convince him otherwise. "They're kids, Dad. The ones that you want me and Ryan to shoot are children."

"Get that out of your head. They're Immundus—the end."

I want to throw something at him. How can he not see how wrong this is? How is he so blind?

"I told you I won't do it."

"I can get the three, sir," Ryan interjects.

"Shut it, Ryan. This is between my daughter and I. She has to learn to get over herself and consider the greater good."

"I am. We have plenty of Immundus. We don't need anymore. There is no greater good to this. I don't even understand why we're out here looking for more we don't need."

He sends me a deadly look. "Drive."

I resume control of the car and speed up to catch the Immundus. Ryan and my dad shoot down all four. I come to a stop so they can load the bodies.

"Get out of the car, Nia." My dad's voice is granite.

I jump out. He hands me the tranquilizer and says, "Load it back up."

I pull one out of the container from the car and load the gun, but I don't understand what point he's trying to make. He's gotten what he wanted.

My dad points to one of the children. "Now shoot that Immundus."

"You already shot it." I stare down my father, then glance at Ryan, hoping he'll intercede. But Ryan just stands there with his head down.

"We're not leaving until you shoot it."

"Why? That makes no sense whatsoever."

"Nia, shoot it." His words become sharper.

I stare at the bodies before me, trying to determine the reason he chose a child, but I don't understand. "Why the child?"

"Because a second dart won't harm the adult, but it will kill the child." His words are razors cutting slits across my heart. How can he ask this of me? Even though I'm out in the open, I feel like I'm suffocating.

My fragile hold on my emotions explodes. "No! I'm not killing a child!"

"They shouldn't be procreating. They are spreading their genes further than we can reach and faster than we can handle. Soon they'll be everywhere. And like you said, we already have too many back at Genesis. So we should exterminate these and be done with it."

"Dad, have you lost your mind? You can't seriously want me to kill this child."

"I want—no, I *need* you to toughen up for this job. There are other things I can and will teach you, but first I need to know that you are willing to kill an Immundus—any Immundus. I need to know that you understand that an Immundus is all they are. They are nothing more, and they are all the same. They are all the same threat to our race."

Images of Fiducia and her torn flesh fill my mind, of Kashmir and his scars and wounds, and the naivety of my words to Kashmir—*We're not murderers*—burrow into my veins. How silly I must have seemed to him—to think that this last line had not been crossed. To think that perhaps imprisonment and torture didn't lead to killing. He was right. I was wrong. And worse, I was wrong because I didn't want to believe it. I attempted to brush it away, to think that perhaps my father was complicated but not unredeemable. There is much more for me to learn, my father says, and I'm guessing next on the list would be torture. In my core, a fiery rage begins to burn. We've all been fed lies, like rancid pills covered with molasses, disguising reality's nastiness. But worse than the lies is what the Immundus have to deal with: abduction, torture, and death. And for what? Because they evolved differently as a result of products my family put on the market, rather than natural order?

I put on the coldest, most clinical voice I can muster. My father does not respect emotion, but maybe he'll respect logic. "Why must I kill her? I do not understand your reasoning."

"You are not qualified to question my reasoning. Kill the *child*, kill that monstrosity, or I will leave you out here all night, several nights if need be. We need to know that you're committed to the cause. We will not tolerate your immaturity or your queasiness any longer. You need to grow up, Genia."

We? Ah, the Domus Council. Even though this is unforgivable, some part of me is glad for the possibility that it's the Domus Council demanding I commit cold-blooded execution, rather than my father alone. It provides a minuscule portion of comfort. He could be trying to save me again—but this time, it does matter. The price is too high.

My father aims the tranquilizer at me, ready to leave me here, alone. Every inch of my body feels like it wants to collapse. My throat lunges into my stomach. Ryan does nothing that might redirect my father to him. I am alone in this.

"No." The moment the word crawls from my mouth, I can barely believe it does. But it's the only answer I'm willing to give. I will not kill an Immundus—not for my father, not for science, not for our species survival. There must be another way to save all of us.

"What did you just say, Genia?"

"I said *no*," I repeat, reaffirming my stance even though I am terrified of the consequence.

My father stares at me. He walks up to me and presses the tranquilizer gun to my stomach. I tremble, but do nothing. What can I do?

After our stare down, he lowers the gun, then aims it to my right and shoots the child himself. I feel a scream scratching at my throat, but I suppress it. I steel myself. I cannot scream. I cannot cry. I cannot react in front of him.

"There will be *no* excuses next time, Nia. None whatsoever. Next time you will shoot and prove your loyalty to our cause, our mission, and to science itself. This is the last time I cater to your childish tendencies and your desire not to get your hands dirty like the rest of us. This is the last time, Nia. Do you understand?"

The last time. Then this will have to be my last hunting trip.

I don't know what I will do, but I will do something.

My father gestures me into the car, furious. I get in.

I came to Genesis to save lives, not take them. Eric's words stitch their way into my skin. *I know that you care about life. That if the way to save our species is by hurting an Immundus, you won't.*

On the drive back to Genesis, I strategize how I can smuggle the Immundus out of the genus. *Freedom*, Fiducia said. I will give that to her, to all of them. Then I will find another way to save my own species—a way that's not paved in death and torture.

I glance over at my father, who is still fuming. I was right. I didn't know him. And now that I do, I wish I didn't. What I'm planning to do will destroy him, but he left me no choice. This is for the greater good—just not his definition of it.

My hands choke the wheel for an instant, before I return to counting cameras.

PART THREE

AND THE LIGHT WAS DIVIDED FROM THE DARK

SIXTEEN

FREEDOM PLAN

The moment I get in my car, I direct Jules to Eric's house, then thrust my head down between my legs and scream. I release every sound that was beating to come out—every terror, every devastation, and every shock. *He nearly made me kill someone. He nearly shot me. And then he killed that child anyway.*

I step out of the car onto the sidewalk in front of Eric's house. The world teeters and my head feels lopsided. Breath is hard to find. After what seemed like hours, I made it to the door, where Eric's affable mother answers. She looks at me with concern, holding my shoulder as she leads me to a seat. The home smells of orange marmalade. She offers me orange juice, which I can't resist.

"I just squeezed it, so it's fresh."

"Fresh-squeezed orange juice? Count me in," Eric chimes, galloping down the stairs.

"Sorry I'm late. I ended up waiting for Jules to pick me up."

"I'm just glad you're here. Is everything all right?" Eric says, folding my hands into his. His wry smile affirms his appreciation of my presence, but his eyes paint over like Mrs. Marcello's. In my periphery I see the beam of Mrs. Marcello's smile. Eric may be her stepchild but I can tell she loves him and wants him to be happy.

"There's something I want to talk to you about." My eyes glide over to Mrs. Marcello's presence. "Can we talk somewhere, please?"

"I know just the place." He helps me up. I must look as bad as I feel. "Mom, we'll be in the atrium."

"Okay, dear."

Releasing one of my hands, he guides me to his home's atrium.

"Your atrium is so beautiful," I say. All houses have atriums at the center, with hallways that lead out to various areas of the house. The entrances to the atriums have transparent shields that enable the home to maintain the optimum environment for the plants and vegetation to grow. The home knows to retract the shields upon our approach. The halls leading to the atrium remind me of spokes on a bicycle. Some houses have more hallways than others, depending on the size of the family—Eric's house has five.

I admire the arrangement of flowers and plants around the outer edge and the Roman fountain in the center of the atrium. There are four benches, with green cushions that melt into the landscape, positioned north, south, east, and west, along the rim of the garden. We sit on the northern seat, farthest away from the hallway entrance that leads to the front room and closer to the hall that leads to the backyard. "Our atrium is just dirt right now."

"That happens when you don't plant anything." He chuckles. His chuckles always come from his stomach, deep and melodic.

"True." The water is soothing as it cascades from the fountain lulling me into contentment. I can sit here for hours listening to the symphony of drops drowning out my thoughts.

"So what is it that you want to talk to me about?"

"I . . ." How do I tell him? "I love you."

I'm stalling and we both know it.

"I love you, too, and I know something's wrong. What is it?" His hand slides down my arm to the tips of my fingers, maneuvering my hand into his and causing cells to dance throughout my body.

I close my eyes and take a few deep breaths. I reopen my eyes and explain everything starting with my ancestors' actions, the hunting expeditions, my failed rescue attempt, what happened today, my father's threat and ultimatum, and I end with my idea: I need to help the Immundus escape the genus, including those who are genus-born. His mouth sits motionless, his eyes drawn away from the moment. I become nervous about his reaction and stand up to pace. He stops me by taking my hand and stands.

"I'm just trying to process everything you told me. Give me a second." He blows out a breath. "What happens after you help them escape?"

"They'll be free and can prepare to protect themselves with their people."

"No, I mean what happens afterward for you?" he asks, his brow furrowed.

"I didn't give much thought to it, but I won't be able to come back. If I do, I'll end up like Derek."

He glances down, resting his chin in his hand, wearing a pensive expression. He stays in this statuesque form for a minute before looking up with compassionate eyes, his lips untwisting.

"You won't do it alone. I'll be with you." He caresses the side of my cheek, sending chills throughout my body. I hold his hand to my cheek for a moment.

"It's too risky for you. To my father, you would be a prize to lock up forever."

"I love your big heart, Nia. I love that you want to help them. And I won't let you do it alone. I think what you hope to do is going to require more than just you and me. In order for us to be safe after releasing the Immundus, we need many people on our side. We need to be prepared to bring Genesis down, so they can't do this anymore."

"I know, but who can help?"

"My mom and dad can help."

"Are you crazy? They'll try to stop us," I say in a hushed tone.

"I am crazy . . . for you," he says, pulling me down the hall toward the front room.

Even now, when we're making plans that could kill us, he makes me grin. "I'll give you that. But your parents? Really?"

He stops, turns, and says with his mellifluous voice, "Do you trust me?" His forehead rests on mine and the love in his eyes reaches into my thoughts. I feel a flutter.

"Yes, of course I do." There is no one I trust as much as Eric.

"Then, please, let me tell my parents. They *can* help us," he reassures me.

I nod, smiling into his eyes, even as an uneasy feeling uncurls deep in my stomach.

· · • ● • · ·

We walk to the front room where we last saw his mom. After getting his mom and dad's attention, he shares with them my tentative desire to help the Immundus escape. I watch in awe how his parents listen to him. They do not interrupt or give any indication of judging me or their son for his willingness to assist me in my endeavor. They sincerely listen. Eric finishes speaking and I pipe up then.

"I don't just have the desire to set them free, I think I might have a plan." Something came to me while watching Eric; I wonder if it will work.

"Before we hear it, when do you plan on conducting this breakout?" Mr. Marcello asks. His voice is calm, yet his crumpled forehead reveals that he is deep in thought or concerned. Could be both. His demeanor is not what I was expecting. His tone is softer than the morning I had breakfast with his family.

"I don't know. Once we assemble the group we can figure that out," I respond.

"And who will be leading this group to which you are referring?"

"I am," I say, waiting for the cackling to begin at the idea that a sixteen year old will lead the charge. It never comes.

"And you?" he asks, staring at Eric. "What will be your role?"

"To support her and help her free the Immundus," Eric says. His mother smuggles in a smile. I sense she's a romantic and proud of the boy she raised.

Mr. Marcello releases a sigh and says, "I think it's about time I share a few things as well."

I nod. He takes in a large breath and begins. "I have a network of friends who want to bring Genesis down. We have been waiting for the right opportunity and you, Nia, have brought that opportunity to us."

"How many people are in your network?" I ask.

"Around fifty. We call ourselves the Liberators," he says, lifting up his sleeve to reveal a tattoo. It's the same tattoo that Oscar has. Mrs. Marcello rubs her hand over her husband's tattoo. Her gesture is cute.

"I've seen that tattoo before. It was on a third-year apprentice. His name is Oscar. Does that tattoo mean that he's a Liberator?"

"His tattoo shouldn't be visible, but yes . . . he is."

"Oh, it's not normally visible. I saw it when he raised his arm and his sleeve fell," I announce in an attempt to exonerate Oscar.

"He's another set of eyes in Genesis along with Maria Matus, Jerrold Tenner, and Jose Esquivel," Mr. Marcello says.

I knew it. I knew Dr. Matus didn't want the Immundus locked up any more than I did.

"Wait! If Dr. Matus is a Liberator, then you already had a chance to save them, yet you did nothing about it. Why?"

"Is this true?" Eric chimes in.

"Yes, it's true. We've wanted to do something for years now but couldn't," Mr. Marcello proclaims.

"Why didn't you just tell people?"

"They wouldn't believe us—not without proof."

"Dr. Matus could have obtained proof. She worked with my dad."

"She didn't join us until *after* she stopped working with your father," he says. "So she doesn't have access to the area they're in. None of our folks on the inside have access to the areas that you do. Now that you are working on his project you can go where he goes. You are the key to bringing Genesis down."

I feel a pang of sorrow for my father, knowing that I'm instigating the demise of his livelihood and family retribution. I wish this didn't have to happen. I wish he could see the Immundus for what they are, sentient like us, just trying to find their way in this world. But he doesn't and he won't—so I've made my choice.

Mr. Marcello propels himself up from his chair and places one arm on his son's shoulder. "Eric, I have a secret that I have been holding on to all these years, because I never knew how to tell you. This isn't the way I wanted to tell you, and I'm sorry, but it's the reason I started this network: to protect you and your legacy."

"What do you mean?" Eric asks, looking as bewildered at his dad's statement as I am.

"The reason Genesis allowed me to keep you and has not bothered us these many years, is because I agreed that when you have children I would give one of them for their research."

"What?" Eric yells, angry yet perplexed. "How could you make a decision that wasn't yours to make?"

"At the time, it was the sole way to walk out of Genesis with you—to save you from that fate. And I knew it would give me time to find a solution. So I built the network, and now with Nia, we can finally prevent it," Mr. Marcello asserts.

Eric runs his fingers through his hair, deep in thought. "What would they want with a child of mine?"

"You're unique, son. The first child of a Homo sapiens and Homo immundus. They want to determine the strength of the Immundus gene," Mr. Marcello says.

"It's not going to happen," Eric mumbles, shaking his head.

"Of course not. Nia, whatever your plan, I know someone who can help. We have a Liberator who works on microchips. He can pull data from the microchip in your hand and we can use that to gain access to the same areas you do. We will need to turn off your locator, though," Mr. Marcello explains.

"That's why my father never bothers to ask where I am going. He can track me," I think out loud.

"Yes, but we have to keep your father believing that he can track you. We won't deactivate it until the day of the freedom mission," says Mr. Marcello.

"I like that. The freedom mission," I reiterate, playing with the tone. That's what Fiducia wants—freedom.

"There's one more thing about the microchips," says Mr. Marcello.

"What?" Eric's tone announces his obvious concern.

"In order to pull the necessary data from the microchip, we will need to cut it out of your hand." Mr. Marcello points to my hand.

I peer down at my palm, wondering how bad the pain could be. I don't even remember it being put in my hand. The mere thought of someone cutting me open sends an electric current throughout my body, causing me to shake.

"Are you okay with that?" Eric asks me.

"There must be another way," Mrs. Marcello chimes in. Her concern for me is endearing. I can see where Eric gets his warm manner. I know that if I want our mission to be successful, they will need my microchip. I don't want to be the sourpuss that starts and halts the efforts of the mission all in one night.

"I'm okay. I can handle it. I can do this." Somehow I feel I'm trying to convince myself rather than the others.

"I know you can." Eric's father places his hand on my shoulder. "You are a hero."

"I'm not a hero."

"You'll be a hero to all the Immundus who you help free."

I never thought of myself as a hero. I doubt I ever will, but I know I am doing what I feel is right. "I guess so."

"It's true. But now that you're privy to this new information—what is your plan?" Mr. Marcello asks.

I suck in a large wad of air, and I tell them.

SEVENTEEN

CHUCK

I can't believe it was just yesterday we told Eric's parents about everything. After I explained the plan, Mr. And Mrs. Marcello told me that I had to embrace my role and accept the reality: I was the leader of this mission and needed to have confidence in everyone else respecting that fact. I wanted to laugh, but Mr. Marcello reminded me that without me, without my access, the freedom mission wouldn't exist. I suppose they're right about that. It is my mission. But it's still hard to believe.

Once we started planning logistics, Mrs. Marcello scheduled the dinner with the Liberators for tomorrow, so Eric and I decided to take advantage of tonight by going to The Colosseum and then to The Spa—a place where we used to hang out with Casey and Alex—for what might be the last time.

Eric called Chuck, one of the gamers who handles the engineering of Spero, to set up a game for us. Over the years, we got to know Chuck as an Immundus sympathizer. One time he even told Alex to stop talking smack about the Immundus because he had no right to talk about a species he never met. Chuck also lost his only son to allagine. Or at least that's what he thinks. His wife died shortly thereafter. He's always allowed us extra time on the field whenever we needed it, so Eric and I figured he wouldn't have a problem setting a game up tonight. We were right.

"Thought I'd never see your faces around here again." Chuck gleams, standing near the player entrance. He's tall and a bit chunky, with a patch of hair on his mostly bald head.

Eric wraps my hand in his. "We're on a date."

"When'd you two hit it off? I thought you were just friends." He lets us in and we trek through the hall.

"We were, but things changed." Eric looks at me, his face practically outshining the lights.

"Wasn't expecting you to be dressed in your uniforms."

"It's for nostalgia and the gadgets that come with the suits. You never know when you'll need them." I was the one who convinced Eric to play Spero in our team jumpsuits.

As we make our way toward the field, Chuck presses buttons on his digital pad. "So, what'll you have: intermediate or hard?"

"What, no basic?" Eric says.

"For you two—no—that's kiddy play."

"Let's go with hard," I say. My body stirs with excitement. I've played this game for years and I want my last time to be worthy of playing.

"You must really miss the action," Chuck says as he maneuvers his index finger from one button to another.

"Yeah, actually, I do."

"Do you want random or do you want me to be a spectator and choose the obstacles for you?

"I don't know. What do you want, Nia?"

"Let's go with random and see what the system comes up with." Just then I remembered that the gamers won the last game and no one even told us that the gamers were playing. "Oh, I've been meaning to ask why no one told us we were playing against you gamers in the last game."

"It was my boss's idea that he wanted to try out. He sent a message to the spectators via their glasses asking if they wanted us to assign a time limit to the game. He told them if the time limit runs out before any team exits, the gamers would win, rather than the teams on the field. It was his way of evaluating us . . . see how good we were at setting up the obstacles. All this happened before you even got your earwraps."

"Well then set us up as a team against you." I glance at Eric, who nods. "How much time will you give us?"

"How about twenty minutes?" Chuck pulls the earwraps and glue from his pocket and hands them to us.

"That works," Eric and I say at the same time. I put the adhesive on my earwrap and put it in place, then hand the glue to Eric who does the same.

The maze takes form and Eric and I get into position at the line near the entrance and wait for the bell. Eric reaches over and gives me a kiss. "I love you."

I grin and take hold of his hand. "Ditto." He smiles because he knows the reference. We watched the movie *Ghost* one night that we binge watched classics. We were friends then, but now I understand that kind of love that transcends existence.

The bell sounds.

We run toward the entrance and a giant wall takes form with a rope dangling from the top.

"Child's play!" I yell out. We scaled walls most mornings before school for our combat training. But I realized I spoke too soon when I noticed something seeping from the top. Eric and I grab the rope and ascend. Halfway to the top, the slippery goo makes it hard to plant my feet on the wall.

"Activate Voice Control 730225." The screen on my forearm flashes, letting me know I have voice control. "Initiate shoe spikes," I say, dangling from the rope. My grasp is not as strong as it was when I trained daily. Maybe I should have taken that into account before choosing a hard level. The shoe spikes take form, and I slam my feet into the wall. I hoist myself up, slamming each foot into the wall to get a good grip. Eric is beside me, doing the same.

We make it to the top and see the whole maze laid out across the field. Just behind the wall and to the left is clear blue water and farther down to the right is sandy land. The water looks farther down than what we climbed.

"Well, what do you think? Jump into the water or fly to the land?" I close my eyes and wait for an answer, which comes quickly.

"Fly. What does your instinct tell you?"

"The same."

"Initiate wings," we say in sync. Extra cloth appears between the arms and legs of our jumpsuits.

"You count us off," I say.

"On three?"

"On three."

"One . . . Two . . . Three."

We jump forward, spreading our arms and legs, sailing through the sky, and maneuvering toward the land. On the ground, I reach over to touch the water and discover that it's actually gelatinous. It would have been much more difficult for us to reach land if we jumped into the fake water first.

"Disengage wings." The extra material disappears.

A hologram appears, along with hurdles on the route before us. "You have fifteen seconds to cross this patch of hurdles." The hurdles don't look so bad, until I notice they start shifting in size. "Begin."

Eric and I easily make it over the first one, but the second one shifts upward the moment I place my hands on it and jump up. My knee hits the top, and I fall down. Eric stops on the other side of it. "Are you okay?"

"I'm good, keep going." I wave him forward as I push myself up. The hurdle drops back down, and I jump over. I see Eric fall ahead when a hurdle shoots up. We both continue forward, falling occasionally. "Five seconds." Eric is done but I have two more hurdles to go. "Three . . . Two . . ." I make it across.

"Great job, you two!" Chuck's voice comes across my earwrap. "You have ten minutes left before I win."

The maze shifts revealing several routes. At the end of each route is a door. "Let's go down the center," Eric says. I nod and follow him. The door opens to a room with a table. The table has a pair of scissors and a three-by-five card. A hologram appears. "Cut a hole in the card that is big enough to put your head through. You have two minutes, beginning now."

Eric picks up the card, rubbing it between his fingers and flipping it around. His eyes are pensive. There is no way we can fit our head through a three-by-five card if we cut a hole in it. Maybe if we cut several holes and then connect them together like a chain. But we have nothing to hold the chain links together.

"I got it." Eric says. "Remember the orange peel belt we made the second year of school." That was the year we took Sustainability. We had a project to make an entire outfit out of food. Eric was on my team. One person on our team had the task of making pants out of potato peels. I'm glad I didn't have that task because I heard it took forever to peel all the potatoes, let them dry out, then sew all the patches together. I made the shoes out of pineapples, after taking out the juicy meat and letting that dry. Eric made the belt by peeling one large orange without lifting the peeler. He ended up with a long coil that we unraveled to become the belt. He used a safety pin to connect the ends.

"Yes, I remember."

"We can do the same thing with the card by cutting a spiral out and then unraveling it."

"Do it."

Eric cuts around the edge first, spiraling his cut until he gets to the center. He stretches it out and wraps it around his head. The maze opens up, revealing one long hall that looks like it has no doors or halls. We run. The hall seems to get longer as we continue running. "Five minutes until the maze shuts down," Chuck announces.

"Stop!" I yell to Eric. "We must be missing something. The hall seems to keep extending."

"Maybe there's a certain point we have to get to before it reveals something." The desire to win sparkles in his eyes. He looks over his shoulder.

"I think it already has and we missed it because we ran past." I can't help but think I saw something. A clue on what to do next.

"What do you mean?" I could tell that he was slightly agitated, knowing the timer was counting down as we spoke.

"I thought I caught something off my peripheral when we were running but when I turned, all I saw was a wall. I want to go back to figure out what it was that caught my eye."

"We're running out of time, are you sure you want to go back?" His tone told me he didn't.

I look past him and then turn to look behind me. "Yes. I know there was something."

"Okay. I'll follow you."

"No, stay next to me. We'll walk briskly, but I want you to look at that side of the wall; I'll look at this side."

"Will do."

We walk back, scanning the walls. We get to a spot where I notice a shift in the lighting. "Stop." I stretch my hand toward the wall and my hand goes past. I step through the wall opening into another hall parallel to the one I was in. The new hall was the same color, which created the illusion that the wall was without openings. But the ends of this hall lead outside the maze. The moment Eric walks through, the maze dissipates.

Chuck's voice comes through the earwrap. "Congratulations! You beat the timer by ten seconds."

"That's because we did it together," Eric says. "I would have kept running."

"And I was stumped on the three-by-five card."

We make our way to Chuck, hand in hand. A calm energy flows through me. Eric and I had never played by working together. Each of us on the team took different routes and handled activities on our own, unless the maze placed us into a room together. But it was nice to have someone else to figure things out with.

"It would be interesting if Spero could be played outside of the stadium," Eric says.

"It could be."

"Really? What about inside of a building that already has halls and different floors?" I ask.

"Sure. We've never done that, so working within a building with many floors would be fun. The players would work their way to the top floor with different levels of difficulty on each floor. We could have floors open up and drop people to another floor or send them down a slide into water. Yeah . . . I like that idea, Nia. Don't know if the managers would like that, though."

"What if we offered you a chance to create a Spero game in a building?" I ask.

"How would we get the spectators involved?"

"There wouldn't be any spectators," I reply. Chuck's eyebrows contort into a state of confusion. "We'd like you to come to a dinner at Eric's house so we can talk to you more about it." I hold my breath. Chuck rubs his chin and contemplates.

"Dinner, you say?"

"Yes, my mom's cooking a big feast."

"Well, I've never been one to turn down a good meal. Count me in."

· · • ● • · ·

After Eric dropped me off at home, I changed, then headed to The Spa to meet back up with Eric. Apparently he got here before me, at least according to the attendant. I place my hand on the door reader to gain access to the private room only we can enter since the system recognizes our chips paid for it. I see him sitting there in the hot tub, eyes closed, arms crossed, his head resting on a pillow. Shadows of candlelight dance along the walls, almost in sync with the serene sounds of nature emanating from the speakers. Warm water wraps itself around me as I lower myself into the bubbling bowl of bliss. Warmth radiates throughout my body as I slink into one of the seats. He doesn't respond to me entering, but the light-blue pulse between his left ear and eye tells me his media chip is on. The seat scans my body, aiming the soft whirl of jets toward my lower back. Ahhh. My frustrations from the day strip from my muscles with every whip of water. I normally would fall asleep, but I can't now. How can I when Eric is seated across from me?

I ogle Eric, as his chiseled chest and speckled abdomen glisten from the soft spray of light. A definite hottie. I guess he always has been; I just never paid attention or saw him shirtless before. And how could I? Every time our Spero team came to The Spa after a game to soothe our muscles, he always had a T-shirt on. I always thought it was weird but wrote it off as an Eric thing. I wade forward and reach for the pulsing light on his temple, to shut off whatever he's watching. Water drips from my hands onto his face before I can reach it.

"What the heck?" He wipes his face with his bicep, turns off his media chip, and opens his eyes.

"Sorry. I didn't mean to wet your face." I shrug my shoulders. "I was trying to shut off your media." A rush of blood heats my cheeks. Fortunately, my skin's medium olive tone minimizes signs of blushing.

"You could've just nudged my shoulder," he says, reaching for one of the towels on the low hanging bar along the wall. He puts in more effort to put the towel back, revealing his full spread of back muscles.

"Yeah, I guess so." I shrug. "What were you watching?"

"Twenty-first century music videos." He smiles and nods.

"I like those videos, too. Who's your favorite artist?"

"Pharrell Williams." He glances at the door at the sound of a snap, but it's just someone in a spa next door.

"Cool. Well, I just wanted you to know I was here, so you can go back to relaxing," I say.

I request a pillow from the room's computer. Once it solidifies, I rest my head back and close my eyes. Even with my eyes closed, I can see the faint flicker of light from the candles. We sit in silence as the bubbles sing their lullaby.

EEUUEEUUEEUU.

The blaring cry of an alarm jolts our heads from our pillows. A holographic video appears above us, in the center of the tub. The newscaster announces an Immundus sighting just outside the walls of our genus. Eric and I shake our heads. We know the truth. We lay our heads back down, soaking up the calm.

I find myself lost in memories this time.

I remember the first game of Spero that Casey, Eric, Alex, and I won.

Right after, we all had naively walked over to the snack bar together as the spectators were leaving The Colosseum. Each of us spent about one hour transferring over our digital signature with our photo to fans wanting to collect badges. Our microchips knew how much information to share. It seemed like everyone watching had badge collectors. Some badges are set up with personal contact information; other badges include more detailed profiles for medical emergencies. I have my photo and signature badge because I don't want to give my contact information.

The spectators also wanted to talk with us, so there we stood listening and responding to their questions. We glanced at each other and could tell from the fatigue in each other's eyes that we were all eager to eat, drink, and relax.

Coach took pity on us that day and made an announcement over the stadium speaker informing all spectators to leave the stadium and that no more badges could be collected since the players had a schedule to keep. We didn't have a schedule, but we appreciated that as soon as he said it, the spectators thanked us for our time and left. That was also the first night that we decided to come to The Spa after every game. So many wonderful memories, bottled up in my mind.

I decide I want Casey to be a part of the plan, so I call her and invite her to Mrs. Marcello's dinner.

· · ● ⬤ ● · ·

The night of the dinner meeting arrives.

The liberators trickle in. When Chuck walks in, Eric greets him and they chat. Minutes later Casey walks in, and we touch palms to greet each other and find a corner of the room to catch up.

"How's Alex?" I ask.

"He's fine. I hate that he's so far away. His hologram is just not the same as having him in front of me."

"Did you tell him what I told you about the Immundus?" I had to explain everything to Casey earlier, since the Liberators are well aware of the truth and I couldn't afford to have Casey freaking out tonight.

"Yes, he thinks you're crazy, you know, trying to help savages and all. But he promises to keep your secret."

"We're the savages." I want to take her to the cells to see how we are treating the Immundus.

"What if it's a trick, Nia? What if it's all an act for you to feel sorry for them?"

"Those aren't your words. They're Alex's."

"He's worried about you like I am."

"It's not a trick. I know it's hard to believe because of all the junk in the news, but it's wrong for them to be used by us to run tests to fix a problem we created." I stare at Casey, hoping some of what I said is sinking in, but she shakes her head in disbelief.

"The food is ready. Please follow me," Eric's house hologram announces.

The table is already set with lemon asparagus on top of wild rice, which we'll all wash down with Mrs. Marcello's amazing apple carrot ginger juice. Everything is so well done, from the presentation of the food to the table décor, which consists of a table runner and a bouquet of flowers picked from her atrium. The dinner is delicious.

After dinner we sit in the front room. Mr. Marcello starts by saying, "Thank you for joining us tonight. Most in this room are well aware of the reason I established the Liberators—to save my son's legacy. We've listened and watched to find our opportunity to hit Genesis hard. But we never found our opportunity. Instead, the opportunity found us."

Then Mr. Marcello turned to me. "Everyone, this is Nia—the person making this mission even possible. She is the daughter of John Luna. And during her first year she has already managed to receive an assignment on her father's team, allowing her the same knowledge and access to the Immundus. Access that we can use to our advantage. She will be leading us in this Freedom Mission. Nia, please proceed."

I stand. "Thank you, Mr. Marcello. I want to share with you a story about my friend, Fiducia. She was ten when what the Domus Council calls 'allagine' hit her. We were playing in the park when she suddenly collapsed, writhing and screaming on the floor in pain as scales burst from her body. I thought I witnessed her death, and for six years I mourned her. I dedicated my life to finding the cure for allagine, and when I started my work at Genesis, that's exactly what I thought I was doing. But then I discovered that allagine wasn't a disorder or even a killer—allagine didn't exist. Instead, the reality was that the Immundus gene activated in some children at the onset of puberty. I realized then that my dear friend was alive, but she was held prisoner by Genesis—for a supposed 'cure' she never wanted—and was being tortured for no reason other than she was an Immundus." I take a breath. Everyone is watching, waiting, wondering, what I'm going to say next. "I'm leading this mission and I'm asking for your help, because I believe there must be a better way. It'll be dangerous, and we may or may not win, but we cannot save our species by hurting another. We've done that throughout history and it got us here, with no living animals and us on the cusp of extinction. They deserve their freedom and their lives as much as we do."

I sweep my eyes across the room, focusing a second on each person, letting the information sink in. Then I grab my schematics and roll it out across the table, placing weights on the corners. I've already marked each camera, door, and elevator, but I take the time to explain the buttons, phrases, and music that have to be used to access various areas. Once everyone understands that portion, I continue with the rest of the plan in detail. By the end of the evening, Chuck is on board, and everyone has an understanding of their role, and they gradually filter out of the Marcello home. All except Casey.

"Nia, oh my gosh. I can't believe you're doing all this. It's a lot. I'm worried about you."

"Don't worry, Casey. I'll be fine, but the Immundus won't be if I don't do this. I've seen what Genesis is doing with my own eyes. I can't stand back anymore and let them suffer. I can't."

"I get it, but I can't join you, Nia."

"Why?" I'm a little surprised. *How is she not convinced?*

"Because if I joined you, I could never come back. And I have to stay here. I have to wait for Alex."

I imagine what it would feel like if I had a choice to wait for Eric or leave him behind forever. I don't know if I could leave him behind—not now. So, even if I don't agree with Casey not helping, I understand her reasoning. "Okay, Casey. But you'll keep this to yourself, right?" I throw her a serious stare.

"I already promised that, Nia. And I'm not going back on that promise."

I hug her for an eternity, realizing I may never see her again. "Goodbye, Casey. I'll miss you."

"Goodbye, Nia. I'll miss you, too. And good luck."

EIGHTEEN

RESCUE

The day of the escape arrives. I convince my father to let me go to work in my car since I haven't driven it for a spell. He consents. After his departure from our house, I ride Jules over to Eric's, where I wait for Thomas with Mrs. Marcello, who makes me feel at ease. I'm sure she knows I need the support. Thomas finally arrives. Thomas is the Liberator who is going to cut out a microchip from my hand. Thomas has black hair and is as tall as the refrigerator.

This morning feels like I'm walking through a haze. I don't regret our plan, and I'm not having second thoughts, it's simply that the reality of it is wreaking havoc on my adrenaline.

We all sit at the kitchen table. Thomas pulls out a shiny silver sphere about the size of an orange from his velvety purple bag. I place my hand palm up on the table at his request, and a digital screen emanates from the sphere. Thomas begins doing something on the screen, and a wide horseshoe-shaped magnet is released from the sphere, landing on my wrist and making it impossible to shift my hand.

"Open your hand and stretch out your fingers," says Thomas.

The moment my hand is outstretched, the sphere sends a small needle into my hand causing immediate paralysis. I panic. "I'm going to need my hand at work," I say, frustrated by this unexpected act.

"Don't worry, you'll be able to move your hand again. I have an antidote I'll give you after I'm done. The injection was needed to numb the area, so you should only feel pressure when I cut into your hand," he explains.

I wish he told me sooner.

"How are you doing?" asks Mrs. Marcello.

"I'm doing fine. I'd prefer if Thomas could let me know in advance what he's doing," I patronize, which isn't smart considering the guy is about to cut into my hand.

"I'm going to cut into your hand now," Thomas says with a sarcastic tone.

Mrs. Marcello gives Thomas a motherly that's-not-nice stare.

A laser shoots out of the sphere and begins cutting my hand. A tiny robot arm extends from the sphere, pulls the microchip from my flesh, and places it into a palm-sized digital box. Various lights dance around the digital box once the lid is sealed. After a minute the robotic arm returns the microchip to my hand. Another laser, this one green, seals up my hand, making it appear as if I were never cut open. Thomas is right: I don't feel any pain. But I don't want him to gloat, so I keep the information to myself.

"Now you're good to go," says Thomas.

"You have everything you need to download to the others' chips?" I question.

"Yes," he replies. "It's also masking you from your father now. I programmed it so Mrs. Marcello can track you." I doubt my father ever tracked me since he's consumed with his work, but I feel reassured by Mrs. Marcello's nod.

I wave goodbye to them as I get in my car and return home.

I know that after betraying my father, I can't ever come back to this house. I walk around stroking the walls and touching every piece of furniture and appliance, trying to somehow take the memory of them with me. Upstairs I sit on the edge of my bed, taking everything in. I remember my mom bandaging a cut I got when I tripped over the front step of our house. I was sitting in this very spot. I examine the room, trying to somehow absorb every image, burn it into my brain, so I will always have it with me—my figurine animal collection, my clothes, my posters, my personal science equipment. After what was probably too long, I head out the door.

Even though I'm not alone on this mission, I feel a nervous sensation in my stomach as I get into my car. With every turn of the vehicle, my stomach is being flung to the other side of my body, nauseating me. I struggle to maintain my composure throughout the ride. By the time I get to Genesis, I want to vomit. I step out of the car reminding myself of how strong I am—who I am and what I believe. I recall sweet memories of my friend Fiducia, who has been imprisoned, sliced, and burned for the sake of science. No more. My father's reign is over. I am the legacy. It's my turn—and the rules are going to change.

· · • ● • · ·

I access the building and head to the unnamed floor. I arrive to the first room and disengage the translucent barrier freeing one of the Immundus. I move room-to-room releasing Immundus. I am able to release ten before security guards arrive with lasers. They come sooner than I thought they would.

My father slices his way through security to get to me, his venom-filled eyes primed for attack. He stands there as if waiting for the right time to strike.

"Take her away!" He pushes the words through his lips, disgust spilling from every syllable.

As the guards drag me away, I see other guards grab each of the newly-released Immundus. "No! Let them go!"

There is one guard on each of my arms—gripping me as though I am a three-hundred pound animal trying to escape. I struggle against them to no avail. My pleas fall on deaf ears.

"Don't you understand? They need to be free! John, Father, listen to me!"

The guards throw me into a cold solitary room with barren walls and no furniture. I imagine this is where they put Immundus who misbehave—although I can't picture an Immundus misbehaving. I slink into a corner and wait. I know it won't be long before my father arrives.

When he does, I heave in a breath, preparing for the confrontation we've always been building up to.

"How could you, Nia?"

"How could I set innocent people free? With little difficulty."

"Those things are not people. I trusted you—my legacy—to do what is required of you to fix the abominations we have created. Instead, you are a righteous loose cannon," he shouts.

Even now, after the ultimatum on the hunting trip, even after he's killed, I want to redeem him. I want to make him understand. Because some small part of me hopes that if he understands, if he is no longer blind to the truth, perhaps he'll change.

"I'm not a loose cannon. Can't you see, John? They're not an abomination. Yes, I understand that we did this, that we are the reason they are this way, but it doesn't mean they need fixing. It doesn't make sense to hurt Immundus in order to help ourselves. We need to identify a way to save both species—to coexist rather than compete. They deserve to live just as much as we do," I say in an attempt to appeal to his humanity.

"They are animals!"

"They are not, even though you're butchering them like they are."

My father stops. A light dawning in his eyes. "This is about our hunt the other day. This is about that one—that child—isn't it?"

"Yes and no. It is about her, but it's about all of them. What you are doing is wrong, no matter your justifications. They are *people*, Father."

"They are no such thing. But let's play your little game, Nia. Let's say we set them free to live with their people. What then? You think everything will be fine? You think they won't retaliate against us for what we've done? Like you said before, we can't change the past," he chides.

"If we ask for forgiveness and send them back home, they won't," I recant.

"You live in a made up world, Genia. They won't forgive us. It's not that easy. History has taught us that."

"Well, if you didn't torture them and run tests on them, it would have been easier," I argue.

"This isn't new, Genia," he says, stressing my real name as if it is a tool of persuasion. "People have been testing on animals throughout history. Didn't you learn anything in school?"

"For the last time, they are not animals!" I scream in total disgust.

"I'm sorry; I thought you were studying to be a geneticist." His words drip with sarcasm.

"What does that have to do with anything?"

"In what kingdom is the Homo immundus?" he reproaches with a smile that could cut my throat.

"Animalia." Each syllable slices through my tongue.

"Well then, they are animals after all."

"But so are *we* . . . I thought after all this time, and after dealing with the aftermath of our Homo sapiens ancestors' mistakes, you would have learned something. You should be called Homo indoctis instead, because I see no wisdom in your actions, just a baggage of fear and hatred."

My father's stare is intense and focused. Perhaps the man I knew as a little girl is hidden somewhere behind his stare. Silent. Trapped. Watching from a distance beneath the shell of his existence.

"Why do you insist on discrediting everything I've worked for? Everything I hoped that you would take on?"

"That is not my aim. My aim is to find a better way to save us—a way without so much death and pain. My aim is to do what's right."

"This project goes beyond me. Didn't you ever think that maybe the other genuses have Immundus as well? You have no idea what you have gotten yourself into," he declares. You're destroying our family name, my career, everything! You're just like your mother!"

"What do you mean?"

My father pauses. "She ruined my life by walking out, and now you have ruined what's left of it by destroying all my work."

"I don't know why my mother left, but I am not ruining you, I'm correcting your wrongs!"

"Listen to me, Nia. I can't let you release the Immundus, and that's final."

"So, what, you're going to keep me in here forever?" I ask the question, but I don't think I'm ready for the answer.

"No, just until I know what to do with you." He turns to walk away.

I shake in disgust. "I thought you loved me once, but I guess that was just a fairy tale."

He spins back around. "Nia—" Just then an alarm sounds. My father's eyes narrow at me.

"Go check the holding cells!" he shouts to the security guards.

· · • ● • · ·

When the door opens, two Liberators shoot the guards with the same tranquilizer guns that my father used on the Immundus. Dr. Matus walks in right behind them.

"Hello, John," she says, poised with a glimmer of revenge in her eyes. But revenge for what, I don't know.

"Maria?" my father says, astonishment prevalent in every crease on his face.

"We're here for your daughter."

They square off: stiff statues, motionless, speechless, dauntless—but my father is the heartless one.

"She reports to me."

"And is that all she is to you? An apprentice?"

"What's it to you? You plan on risking your job for her?"

"Somebody has to. And I'm tired of this job anyway."

"It's not me she needs saving from, Maria. Do you think I would hurt my own daughter, my legacy?"

"I've seen what you're capable of John, so no, I have no doubts that you would hurt your own daughter." Dr. Matus's comment confuses me because my father has been trying to keep me safe from whoever hurt Derek.

My father's chin sinks into his chest for a moment, then rebounds. "How did you even get down here?"

"Nia gave us access," Dr. Matus says with a wicked smile.

I can feel the heat from the fire burning in his eyes.

"This is her plan. She rallied over sixty of us to help her and used herself as a diversion to pull you away, while we rescued the Immundus. Your trophies are on their way home, and you're not going to stop them," Dr. Matus says, waving me toward her with one hand, the tranquilizer gun in the other.

I step forward, but my body is whisked back, my neck surrounded by my father's brawny arms. This is the John that Dr. Matus knows.

Dr. Matus raises her gun. "You said you wouldn't hurt your daughter."

"How could you do this to me, Genia? This level of deceit—of betrayal," my father says through gritted teeth.

Dr. Matus moves forward.

"I will break her neck," my father says, squeezing tighter, a python killing its prey.

My arms tremble, too weak to pull his arm away. I can't speak. My airway is constricting, and I'm gasping for air. I manage to squeeze out, "Father. Don't." It's nothing more than a whisper in the middle of a storm.

"I was wrong. She isn't my daughter. My daughter wouldn't betray her father like this. My daughter wouldn't abandon me the way her mother abandoned us."

The memory of the photo he placed on my desk of him, my mom, Faith, and me flashes before my eyes. Although I try to be strong in this moment, a lone tear escapes my right eye and flees down my cheek, landing on my father's arm.

It's then that my heart shatters into a million fragments like glass flung to the floor with no regard. I knew I would be hurting him by freeing the Immundus—I knew he'd be furious. What I failed to account for was the depth to which I would inflict pain.

His grip tightens. I stare at Dr. Matus, wondering if she might get the shot in too late. Black spots appear before my eyes. I close them for a brief moment and hear the swish of the needle rush past me, hitting my father, who crashes to the ground.

I gulp in air, choking on it. Was my father going to *kill* me, his daughter? Did I cause that much anguish or did my betrayal remind him too much of my mother's abandonment? Or worse yet, is there simply no humanity left in my father? I don't know, but part of me, that part that has wanted nothing more than to be a daughter he noticed all these years, is sorry. That part of me hopes he can forgive me—and see the error of his methods. The rest of me is in shock. I never thought I would incite so much hate as to cause him to want to end my life. There must be something that I'm missing. Unless his work means more than my life?

Just as my shock is turning to fury at the idea, Dr. Matus places her hand gently on my shoulder.

"We have to go, the others are waiting for us." Her voice is urgent, yet I can hear the compassion in it. I nod and motion for her to lead the way.

We make it down the hall, but a tranquilizer flies around one of the corners. Dr. Matus hands me a tranquilizer gun. "You know what to do with this. I've seen you play Spero."

In my mind, shooting holographic opponents is much different than aiming at a real body. I could accidentally hit the eye or a nerve, causing real damage. But the bombardment of laser bullets from the Genesis security guards shakes me into the realization that it is either them or me. My heart spins; I reach my arm into the hall, firing tranquilizer shots. Dr. Matus and the two other men with her press forward through the hall, so I follow. One of the men follows behind me. Once we make it across the hall, I look back at the silent bodies littered across the floor. Though they look dead, there's some comfort in knowing that they'll wake up after we're gone. We're not aiming to cause death—that was my rule.

We make our way down one of the halls that held Immundus. I am relieved to see the cells are empty.

"Where are Eric and the others?" I ask.

"We're going to meet them in your father's lab. Chuck has holograms defending the door to the lab so everyone can make it down the elevator safely," Dr. Matus says.

One of our men opens the door to the parking garage. Shots ring through, hitting the man in his chest, arm, and leg; his body now lying to the side of the door. Another laser bullet skids off Dr. Matus's leg, slicing through her skin, sending blood flowing. She applies pressure. I reengage the door. We're stranded. I call Eric, alerting him to our situation. Our other man stands by the door ensuring no one comes through.

"You two are going to have to continue without me," Dr. Matus says. She uses the wall to lower herself to the ground.

"I'm not doing that. You came for me, and I'm going to make sure you make it out of here." I tear off a piece of my shirt.

She cringes, and a slight chuckle creeps forth. "You remind me of your mother."

"How?" I ask as I kneel down and wrap her leg.

"She was caring and compassionate, too. She also wanted to free the Immundus."

"She knew about the Immundus?"

"Yes, she did."

"Did she know about allagine?" I ask.

"Yes."

I don't know what to say. I can barely process this information. "She knew and she left me here with him?"

"She left because she couldn't stay, and she didn't want to go up against your father—she wanted to protect you from that war," she says, groaning. I tighten the strip against her leg. "She had nowhere to run that would be safe for you. She loved you, Nia. She really did."

I nod, tears rising in my eyes. I swipe at them.

"And Nia? She'd be proud of you."

The drum of laser bullets beating on the door interrupts us. I wait to receive a call from Eric telling me it's safe to come through the door, but all I hear are bullets on the other side.

"What's your name?" I ask the man guarding the door.

"Stephen," he says.

"Stephen—can you please help me get Dr. Matus up?"

"Of course."

Stephen and I lift Dr. Matus to her feet, her arm draping over Stephen's shoulder and his arm supporting her waist. Suddenly, Dr. Matus raises her gun. I spin around and see three guards—all armed.

"Drop the gun and come with us, Nia, or we'll kill these two. And Dr. Matus, don't think about shooting any tranquilizers. You won't bring us down before we kill you." The guard's voice is rough. My head burns and pulses with the decision in front of me. If I try to fight, one of the guards will kill Dr. Matus and Stephen. If I go with them, I may never see Eric again. I know the only chance I have of saving my companions and returning to Eric is if I go with the guards and fight them once Dr. Matus and Stephen are out of sight.

"I'll go with you." I place the gun on the floor and step forward slowly. One of the guards grabs me and pulls my arms behind me, tying a rope around my wrists. I've never fought without arms, but I guess there's always a first time. I follow them down the hall and around the corner. I see a call coming through from Eric. It stops, then rings a second time, then a third. My heart sinks into my chest.

"You're a disgrace and don't deserve to wear the Genesis lab coat," says the security guard holding my arm. I say nothing. He squeezes my arm, pinching a muscle, and I want to yell, but I hold it in.

A man and woman in black suits stand at the end of the hall. I need to free myself before I get to them. I have to hurt the guards.

"Initiate shoe spikes," I say, kicking the guard in front, sending spikes through his back. Whirling to the side, I stomp my feet into the feet and calves of the guards next to me. "Disengage." I run away from them back to my salvation.

"Grab her!" I hear a voice scream in the distance.

I nearly stumble when two holograms appear before me, blocking my path.

"Continue running, Nia. We are here to protect you," the hologram says.

Chuck. I run even faster to make it past the holograms, who are also running toward me.

I see laser shots fly by, barely missing me. They want me dead, after all. I make it past the holograms and turn the corner.

Eric is standing at the door where Stephen stood just a moment ago. My breath leaves me in a rush as I continue running toward him and fall into his arms.

He unravels the rope from my wrists, which are now sore and bruised, hugs me, then presses his lips to mine. "I'm glad you're safe. I knew when you didn't answer something was wrong. I had my mom locate you, then told Chuck where to send the holograms."

"Where's Stephen and Dr. Matus?" I ask, hoping they made it out safely.

"They're on their way to your father's lab." He opens the door.

Our pathway through the garage to the lab is riddled with bodies from our side and my father's side. I try not to think about the dead bodies on our side, but the fragments of my heart cut into my stomach. I tie up my emotions and sling them over my back—a burden I will continue to carry—as we make our way to the elevator. Dr. Matus and Stephen are waiting inside. I play the tune to get us to the level where we can exit. Just as the elevator doors shut, shots puncture the door.

"Ready to blow up the elevator once we get off?" Dr. Matus asks.

"Yes. I don't want them to the exit the genus and re-collect the Immundus or come after us," I respond.

"Jonathon brought the explosives," Eric says. He sends a message to Jonathon to be at the elevator entrance with the explosives.

"We have to let the others know we're about to blow it so they can brace themselves," I say.

"We won't have time, but they'll be fine. They're farther away than we are by now," Dr. Matus replies.

The elevator opens to the tunnel that leads out of the genus. We exit and Jonathon rushes in, placing the explosives in the elevator. The rest of the group and the Immundus have already started the long trek on foot up the corridor. Jonathon stayed behind to provide the explosives. We get into my father's vehicle to catch up with our group.

"Drive!" Eric says.

"It's an antique. It doesn't know anything. You have to drive it manually." I swing up into the driver's seat. "Good thing I know how."

I press the "on" button and start driving us up the corridor. I play my mom's song to reveal the exit doors, and as soon as we are a good distance away, Jonathon sets off the explosives. The boom resounds throughout the tunnel.

Several feelings take hold, an amalgamation of triumph and fear for the most part. I stare wide-eyed at the landscape around us. Far ahead, the Immundus and our group parade toward the light that for the Immundus means freedom, but for me and the other genus-born means a world of uncertainty.

NINETEEN

EXODUS

A sheath of darkness envelops us—the moon and stars hidden from our eyes. It is one of the darkest nights I've ever seen. A menacing fog crawls over the mountains, its tendrils reaching the valley floor. Eric recognizes my discomfort and holds my hand in an attempt to assuage my fears, but to no avail. We drive through the open landscape following behind the Immundus and Liberators. The Immundus home is not as close as I expected, we've been driving for ten hours and have yet to arrive. Eric brings the vehicle to a halting stop to avoid hitting the now stationary group in front of us.

By the light of our vehicle, I see Kafira approaching. The glowing eyes of the other Immundus are on her, curious as to her reason for stopping our caravan.

"We must rest. It is a half day's walk to our town," Kafira says.

"Is it safe to stop here?" Dr. Matus asks.

"Safe?" Kafira pauses for a moment, glancing toward the faint huddled mass. "Do you see cages? Or beds with straps—lying in wait to ensnare us?"

"No," Dr. Matus says, her face revealing the story of a past she can't conceal. "But it doesn't mean that they won't come after us."

"We are safe here, amongst the cover of nature. They have never come so far. You, however, may experience discomfort being outside your temperature-controlled genus. Earth does not regulate her temperature for us."

Mr. Marcello decides to chime in. "We came prepared with tents and blankets. We knew we would be in need of environmental protection."

"So it's agreed. We'll stay here for the night," I say.

Eric reaches out his hand toward me to help me out of the vehicle. Our cadre pulls together, preparing tents for everyone. Mrs. Marcello invites me to share a tent with her and her daughters. I happily accept the invitation. Mrs. Marcello grabs a tent marker from one of the bags, programs the size, and then places it on the ground. Within a few seconds, our tent materializes.

Before I step inside, I scan the area for Fiducia. I found her in the crowd a few minutes after we exited, but I have yet to speak with her. With each footstep toward her, my throat tightens. She was my best friend—until my father's lies separated us. Does she blame me for her captivity under my father's care? We didn't have time to talk about that—to talk about anything really. I only had time to ask her the question that led us here. I sit down beside her, both of us silent for a brief moment.

"I thought you were dead," I say.

"I wouldn't be seated next to you if I were dead," Fiducia replies.

"I know." I gulp. "I didn't know my dad took you for his experiments. I didn't even know about the experiments until I began work at Genesis. I wanted you to know that."

"My mother never came to get me," she says, ignoring my statement. Her eyes glaze over.

"She didn't know either. Everyone thinks allagine kills children. They don't know that you just changed a bit." I pause, hoping for a response. "Remember walking to the park with me?"

"Yes."

"I saw you transform. I thought I was witnessing your death. It wasn't until some days ago that I even went to the park because it would bring back memories of that horrible day."

"I remember, too," she says, in a solemn tone. She glances at me thoughtfully, then turns her gaze toward a nearby tree. "I woke up in a small room . . . confused . . . and shouting for you."

"Did you know I wasn't there?"

She sighs. Her eyes fall upon the ground. "Your dad walked in and told me." She grabs a twig at her feet and draws spirals in a dirt patch—they remind me of DNA strands. "I didn't know I changed until he told me to look at my arms. I guess I was in shock."

"That's understandable," I say in what I hope is a comforting tone.

"I asked for my mom, but he said I could never see my parents again because I belonged to his lab. I hoped, though, that they would come for me," she laments. "Now I'm free but incapable of seeing them. That's what you meant by your question, wasn't it? That you could try to revert me like your father wanted or you could free me, but that I wouldn't see my parents again either way." Her hollow eyes wrought with pain. A pain I understand too well.

"That's not what I intended when I asked it. I just wanted to know what you wanted most—to be Sapiens or be a free Immundus. I wanted to know if you even wanted to change back. I wanted you to have a choice in it." I sigh. "I'm sorry for what my father put you through." I focus on her eyes. "Your transformation was not a reason to take you from your family. I'm sure they would have loved you regardless of your appearance, Fiducia."

"You really think they would love me like this?"

"Yes. I do."

As we talk, her voice changes from rigid to fluid—opening up about her life. I dare not share with her anything that might cause her to realize the experiences she missed from being locked up these many years.

I hear Eric's voice and glance over my shoulder. I smile at him, then return my attention to Fiducia. "Do you remember Eric, Fiducia?"

"Yes, of course. I didn't recognize him until you said his name, though. The years have really changed him."

I suppose she's right, I've just always seen him. "Well, he's my boyfriend now, if you can believe that." I let out a smile before I get to my point. "But what I really wanted to tell you was that his mother is

Immundus and his father is Sapiens. He's a first of his kind—a merging of both our species."

"Eric? But he didn't transform. And he looks Sapiens," Fiducia says.

"I know. But if he wasn't wearing a shirt right now you would be able to tell. Some of his skin is like yours."

"And you're willing to be with him?"

"Yes, I am. His outside doesn't matter as much as what's on his inside. I'm amazed you would think that it would be an issue for me."

"Well, I don't know the person you've become."

"At least now we have the chance to get to know each other again."

"I don't know who I am." Fiducia returns to drawing circles in the dirt. "It's hard to discover yourself while locked in a room. How do you uncover your likes and dislikes?"

"I'm sorry."

"You keep saying that," she says, befuddled. "Please stop. It's not your fault."

We continue talking until we notice everyone around us is heading to sleep. Eric struts over to us, his crooked smile capturing my attention. The sun has yet to wake fully, but the peeking rays create a lambent sky. His approach sends a flurry of warmth to the center of my chest. The sparkle in his eyes is delicious to behold. My face feels flush with excitement that somehow washes away all the troubles on my mind. Fiducia says hello to Eric, who immediately wraps her in a giant hug.

"Hello to you, too, Eric," she says, laughing.

"It's good to see you, Fiducia."

"And you. But I have a question. Can you lift your shirt for me?"

Eric looks between us, confused, before understanding dawns. "You want to see my skin? Sure."

I feel a bit embarrassed for him, but, as always, he's gracious enough to accommodate her request.

"You are a mixture of us!" Fiducia exclaims.

"Indeed, I am. But now, I need to drag Nia off to bed. My mother commanded me to collect and deliver her safely."

We all say goodnight and promise to have breakfast together in the morning.

When I step inside Mrs. Marcello's tent, I see she has set the temperature to a nice seventy-eight degrees.

A luminescent reflection on our vehicle shines through the tent, making it difficult initially for me to fall asleep, but after I turn toward Audrey, Eric's sister, and listen to the rhythmic sound of the trees rustling in the wind, I quickly fall into dreaming.

· · ● ● ● · ·

I wake to the crackling sound of fire harmonizing with Kafira's voice and the hum of nature. The scent of garlic penetrates my nasal passages, perking my eyes. I sit up and notice I am the lone person awake in the tent. I hear the rush of feet exiting tents and picture a herd of people descending upon Kafira. I hear her invite the people to eat, so I get up, grab my bag, and head to the washing station at the southeast edge of our camp. Once presentable, I head to the center of camp to indulge in the sweet-smelling concoction that Kafira prepared. It looks like potatoes. I spot Fiducia and then Eric, and we eat together, chatting happily.

Dawn has yet to break by the time we're off again. While it would be nice to rest, we can't linger too long. We won't feel safe from Genesis until we arrive at the Immundus village.

I opted to walk for a while as Eric drove his mother and sisters in the car.

"If your town is half a day's walk from here, how is it that my father was able to catch so many Immundus near Genus Guadiam?" I ask Kafira, who I've ambled up to.

"We are seed gatherers, charged with gathering seeds beyond our town. We collect and log them," she responds. "The seeds closest to your genus are purer than the seeds near our town, so the seeds are worth the walking trip."

"But why do you need to collect them?"

"Our town is a farming community. We provide food not only for us but for the metropolitan communities. For the last thirty years, our crops have had problems growing. We discovered that the less genetically modified the seed, the more successful the crop."

"Why don't you use the seeds produced by the good crops, rather than return to pick more seeds?"

"We have tried. Although the seeds produce a plentiful harvest, the seeds produced by the plants are damaged by the soil. The very thing that nurtures and houses the plants is the very thing that poisons it."

"How often do you collect seeds?" I ask.

"Every day. We take turns making the trip."

"Didn't anyone wonder why you didn't return? Why didn't they try to rescue you?"

"Those that sought us were also captured."

"Oh."

"You've changed that now, Nia," Kafira reminds me before an Immundus man calls out her name and she walks toward him.

After walking around five miles, my body feels sticky and wet. Beads of sweat congregate on my forehead. I find it odd how the weather changed drastically in five miles, from the moderate and comfortable temperature to this unbearable sweltering heat. I miss the weather-controlled environment of our genus. Curious how the Immundus' bodies reacts to this weather, I jog up to Kashmir.

"So how are you adjusting to this weather?" I say, wiping my forehead with the back of my hand.

"You forget. There is no adjusting for me. This is the world in which I was raised and to which I am accustomed. The adjustment for me resided in my experience in Guadiam," Kashmir says, his eyes fixated ahead. He doesn't even glance once at me.

"Did I do something to offend you?" I watch his profile, hoping to discover an inkling of expression and reflecting on what I might have said or done to cause him to be standoffish toward me.

"Why do you presume that you have done something wrong?" he asks in monotone.

"Well, because you're not looking at me when you talk."

"I was not aware that looking at you was a requirement to speak to you," he says, glancing my way. "I am more than happy to accommodate your request. After all, you saved us."

My face becomes flush. "It was a group effort," I say, shaking my head and sending sweat soaring into the air.

"Yes. But the idea had to start somewhere." His eyes are intense just then. "Thank you, Nia." I feel intense joy. This is the first time he has said my name and part of me feels that perhaps we are beginning to build a bridge of friendship.

I smile. "You're welcome, Kashmir."

My father's vehicle is now in front of Kashmir and I. Eric's head spins around as he searches me out of the crowd that's falling behind. A large smile envelops my face, revealing my teeth. He misses me already, I think to myself.

After a few more miles, an agrarian town becomes visible. Several yew trees line the path to a nearby crop on the outskirts. Its appearance is similar to my genus but without the encumbrance of a monstrous bordering wall.

"What do you call your town?" Mrs. Marcello inquires from the jeep. Her eyes gleam as they dance from site to site, capturing all that is before us. I can tell she is as intrigued as I am—I imagine we all are, based on the wide eyes abounding on the faces of the group.

"Repute," one of the male Immundus announces. "Our city was so named as a result of the good reputation we established with the Metros."

"Metros?" I ask, sweeping my outstretched fingers along the necks of wheat.

"The ones who live in the metropolitan areas—the ones for whom we provide sustenance by way of the food we grow in these crops." Oh. I guess that somewhat makes me a metro, if I had to compare.

"What do they call people from your town?"

"Farmers," the man replies with a grin.

"That makes sense." My dry, embarrassed throat chokes on the words.

A congregation of bodies begins to form at the town's edge—no doubt curious about this herd approaching them. One of the townsfolk begins running toward us. Could it be a family member or close friend of someone in our group? As the person draws nearer, he stretches his vibrant-colored arms and wraps them around a woman whom I don't know. Hugs are apparently universal.

Keen to our differences, those of us who are Homo sapiens congregate, unsure about the treatment we're about to receive now that *we* are the outsiders. Kafira leads us to a large circular building with fleurs-de-lis incised around the outside border. The entrance doors are mahogany with engravings of Homo immundus, some with wings like a hummingbird. I think the depiction of an Immundus with tiny wings is odd—so different from the large-winged angels in my culture. The script *One who serves the Earth serves oneself* adorns the section of wood above the doors.

Three Immundus—Kafira, Kashmir, and another who calls himself Joolya—enter the ornate round building. The others depart their own ways, including Fiducia who motions to me that she'll wait out here for us. Our group of Homo sapiens follows Kafira. I feel the mesmerized gazes of those in the building examining every step we take upon our approach. Six individuals are seated behind a mahogany desk that matches the exterior of the building. I admire the craftsmanship of the table. It's thick and strong, much more durable than what I had in my home. There must be carpenters or artists in addition to farmers in this town for them to have so many wooden structures with intricate designs. All three Immundus approach the table. We wait near the center of the room at Kafira's request.

The lips of each Immundus move in a machinated fashion—voices inaudible—I can only suppose at what is being said. Soon after, we are directed to the table. "You have saved the lives of our people from torture and in so doing, have lost your own livelihoods. Is this not so?" says one of the leaders seated at the table, his eyes streaking across ours. He is the only one at the table with facial hair, which offers him a sense of distinction.

"Nia has saved their lives. This was her plan, and without her it would not have been possible," says Mr. Marcello. Eric winks at me, warming my heart.

"And who is this Nia?"

I take a step forward, hesitant to speak. "I am."

"Thank you, Nia. We are indebted to you for the kindness shown to our people. You are welcome to stay here—as is your group. We will make provisions for you." An Immundus to the leader's right whispers in his ear. "I would be delighted to have you as our guests for dinner. Would you bestow us this honor?"

The others in my group give me nods in acceptance. "Yes, we would be delighted," I respond.

"Guest quarters will be presented to you by Jashway until suitable living arrangements are identified in Patmos, the nearest metro area. He will also show you where dinner will be held," says the Immundus to the right of the leader. "At dinner, you will also meet the Patmos envoy, who is responsible for resettling individuals in the metros to best suit their skills. She was visiting Repute to check in on the abductions situation, and now we will have good news for her indeed."

I smile and we thank them for their kindness and generosity before following Jashway to our temporary residences. We walk through town, and I can't help but wonder what will happen to me and where I will go—where will they resettle me in the metros? Will any of my schooling be useful in this new world?

· · • ● • · ·

The town is small compared to Genus Guadiam, so walking from house to house shouldn't feel so exhausting, but the sticky heat is becoming so unbearable that I shed my top shirt, revealing my damp tank top. We arrive to the place Fiducia and I are staying. We opted to stay together and to stay near Eric's family, who get a house to themselves. The light gray walls remind me of Genus Guadiam. Posts with fabricated butterflies at the top line the walkway to the dark cherry door. The creak of the door announces our arrival. I place my hand up to keep the door open, following Jashway into the house. I strain to keep it open long enough to walk through. The room has burnt red shelves lined with an assortment of books, some tattered and some that still maintain their sheen and perfect edges. I make out the classics of *Jane Eyre, The Sun Also Rises, The Book Thief,* and *Merlin Unmasked* before Jashway directs us to the right where a large semi-circular sofa hugs a circular light bamboo table—the same color as the bamboo flooring in my home. I clear my throat, keeping my emotions bound. I attempt to redirect my attention so I don't focus on the home I left.

The inside is larger than I expected from the exterior of the house. I feel small standing under the vaulted ceiling. We walk down the hallway that leads from the foyer to the back of the house.

"This is a beautiful house," Fiducia announces.

"Thank you," Jashway responds.

"Who lives here?"

"You do for now. The home belonged to an Immundus family who went missing and did not return with your group, so I imagine they are among the many that lost their lives there." My heart is stabbed by his words, knowing that I am staying in the home of a family that my father most likely tortured and killed. I bandage my heart and tie the words to everything else that weighs me down.

"This is the first house I've been in since becoming an Immundus." I'm drawn to Fiducia's thankful eyes, and watch her scan the house, inch-by-inch, taking it in as if she were afraid to lose this moment.

Pictures line the hall that lead from the foyer to another room toward the back. I feel better knowing of their existence, of what the owners looked like, before I stay in their house. Like at least there is some way of knowing them, even if they are gone.

Our bedrooms are at the back of the house. Jashway leaves after showing us around the house, and Fiducia and I choose our rooms. I sit on the bed and reflect on what transpired these last few days. My heart aches, recalling the last time I saw my father—his anger, his disgust, his rage, and his attempt at killing me. I stay in my melancholy until Fiducia walks in, lifting the corners of my mouth.

"Jashway said we could help ourselves to any clothes that might fit us, right?" Fiducia says.

"Right."

"Are you going to dinner in what you're wearing now or are you changing?"

"I don't know yet." I jump from the bed and head to the closet to figure out the clothing options. I bang into the doors. My face is hot from embarrassment. "I guess these doors aren't like the ones back at our genus." I discover a button that manually opens the doors. We thumb through the variety of multi-colored dresses, skirts, pants, and blouses.

"So what do you think is in this city?" Fiducia says, taking a seat on a blue sofa opposite the bed.

"A guy for you," I respond, immediately thinking of Eric and already missing him. She giggles like an infant learning to laugh for the first time—it warms me like a cup of herbal tea. "And . . . I hope we will find doors that open automatically and cars that drive themselves."

It's funny how I took for granted the things I thought were so simple. I see the happiness in Fiducia's eyes and discover the girl I once knew, as though time shifted and we never spent time away from each other. I respond to Fiducia's questions regarding the world we left behind making sure not to glamorize anything.

After around two hours of talking, I glance at the time. "Oh my gosh! We have fifteen minutes to get dressed and to dinner," I announce.

Fiducia grabs an outfit and scampers to her room. I pull an emerald green shirt and brown pants from the hanger and get dressed. We all make our way to the foyer at the same time and rush out the door, only to encounter Eric, leaning against the fence, and Jashway right behind him.

"Eric."

I look at him and everything fades to nothingness, except for the ptunk, tunk, tunk of my heart. That is, until Fiducia's voice filters through.

"See you two at dinner!" Fiducia winks at me and scampers ahead to Jashway.

Eric looks at me intently, and I feel my skin warming. Before I can think, he pulls me into his arms, his lips on mine, and I'm filled with a bright burst of joy. I hadn't even realized how much I'd needed this.

"Sorry," Eric whispers against my lips. "I just couldn't wait one more second to do that."

"I think I understand the feeling," I reply on a sigh.

We embrace for a moment before I pull away, my cheeks pulled up in a smile. "We better start heading to dinner."

"Ah, I see. I forgot about your love affair with food." I lightly punch him in the arm. "No worries, I had Jashway show me where dinner would be held so I could take you there."

"Well, don't forget again. I like to be fed. *On time.*"

"Good thing I can cook, then, and quickly, too," he says, chuckling, and in that moment, I love him so much it hurts. Without even thinking, I swiftly kiss him again, surprising him, before jogging away.

"Come on, slow poke!"

He laughs a full belly laugh and follows me.

At the house we are greeted by one of the leaders who we met already. The scent of mint, rosemary, and thyme fills the air. We take our seats.

Then the leader, who announced himself as Ashafton, clears his throat. "Nia." I snap to attention. "Welcome. Before we feast, I'd ask you to stand and share the purpose for which you chose to help our people. Though, I am sure the entire tale will be heard in time, it is the purpose in which I am interested, so that we may toast to it."

Part of me thinks it's an odd request, but then I remember how important the *why* and my reasoning has been to all the Immundus men and women I have met. They are a culture driven by intention as much as action.

I stand and carefully measure my words. "Your people did not deserve to be captured and used as test subjects against their will. We are all people. We are all part of the same human race. And all deserve to live free," I explain. Ashafton stares at me for a moment with a half-smile, his lips so thin they seem like threads sewn from dimple to dimple. Then he nods his head.

"So it is. To the heart of Nia, the leader of the Liberators, who saw injustice where others did not." He raises his glass and we all toast; I am sure I'm blushing beet red throughout it.

"You are our people and are welcome to stay as long as you wish. Please, feast upon all manner of food that we have prepared for you." He points to one of several men and women walking in with trays of food. The cornucopia of color emblazons my eyes. The smells—intoxicating. I am eager to devour what they set down.

I'm about to sit down when Ashafton exclaims, "Ah! Envoy! There you are!" Ashafton looks over my shoulder toward the entrance of the room. "You just missed this young leader's wise words. Come, meet her, as we settle in to eat." Ashafton motions toward a figure in the doorway, and I turn toward it.

A Homo sapiens woman enters the room. I wasn't expecting any Homo sapiens to be living outside of the genuses. I pull my shoulders back, straightening up, ready to meet this envoy who will determine our relocations. She reminds me of my mother, the way her hair falls against her face and the way she moves across the room. She's a few feet from me when our eyes meet. She stops suddenly, dropping a tablet from her hands. Even if her olive complexion is now pale and her chestnut hair is now frayed, her eyes haven't changed—not in all the years she snuck out of my life. I'd know them anywhere.

"Mom?"

· · ● · ·

WANT EVEN MORE?

Connect with Christina Enquist online!

www.christinaenquist.com

eBook edition also available

CHRISTINA was raised in Salinas, California and developed a love of storytelling at an early age. While she's been dreaming up stories her whole life, she only recently started to transfer all of the worlds she's created to the page. Aside from writing, she works full-time and spends as much time as she can writing stories and enjoying time with her husband, dog, and cat.

Christina lives in Visalia, California with her family. *The Immundus* is her debut novel. You can visit her at

www.christinaenquist.com.